The Barnstormer

by

Jane Lewis

The Barnstormer

Cover Art by *Debbie Taylor*

The Wild Rose Press, Inc.
PO Box 708
Adams Basin, NY 14410-0708
Visit us at www.thewildrosepress.com

Publishing History
First Vintage Rose Edition, 2018
Print ISBN 978-1-5092-2221-6
Digital ISBN 978-1-5092-2222-3

Published in the United States of America

Dedication

To my sister, Margaret, for encouraging me to always follow my dreams. Her love and stories of a small Georgia town bring laughter and tears and inspire me every day.

Chapter One

Saplingville, Georgia, 1936

Frankie Howard pulled into the parking lot of Andrews Airfield and parked beside his boss's car. He sat in his Model A, a death grip on the wheel. Bitch, gold digger, and slut played through his mind like a reel at the picture show.

He stared at the hangar and imagined punching his fist through the window and kicking a hole in the wall.

Victor, his boss and best friend, came out the door and walked toward his car.

He got out, opened the trunk, and handed the boss a box of motor oil.

"What took so long?" Victor placed the box beside the door and took one look at his friend. "Holy shit, what happened to you? You look like the New York Giants after they lost the World Series."

Frankie bent over at the waist and placed his hands on his knees for support. Air forced into his lungs in small short breaths. He inhaled one long breath and straightened. He staggered back and leaned against his car.

Victor walked toward his friend and stared. "For God's sake, tell me what happened."

He stepped to the side making space between them. "That bitch, Audrey, used me. She was married when we got married. I'm an idiotic, stupid fool. She played me like a fiddle at a Saturday night dance. Son of a bitch."

Victor shook his head in disbelief. "Sorry man. How'd you find out?"

He relaxed his jaw. "The jerk was at my house, my house. In my bedroom. With my wife. I wanted to kill the bastard. I roughed him over and kicked him out. He went straight to the sheriff's office. Deputy Riley came to my door, hauled me and Audrey in."

Victor spoke, "What happened then?"

His eyes locked with his best friend, a sense of worthlessness swept through him. "She chose him. She chose him over me. Why'd she marry me in the first place?"

Victor placed his hand on Frankie's shoulder. "I tried to tell you, but you couldn't see past her looks. She was all about the airplanes, and the trips, and the money she thought you had."

He felt boxed in, he needed the sky. "Help me ready the Jenny."

Victor grabbed his arm. "I can't do that. You're in no shape to fly an airplane."

He clenched his fists. If Victor wasn't his best friend, he'd punch him out. "I'm. Fine."

Victor stepped in front of him. "We've known each other since we were kids. I've never seen you this upset. Go in the hangar and calm down, then take the Jenny up."

He walked toward the grassy field and turned. "I'm all right, or I will be once I'm in the air. You gonna help me or not?"

Victor shook his head. "You're as stubborn as Uncle Walter's mule."

They walked toward the pasture. He stared straight ahead. "Do me a favor, tell Al all this shit."

Victor walked behind him. "I'll tell him as soon as I get back to the hangar. I don't think he'll be surprised."

He walked faster. "I'm sure everyone in town knows by now." He reeled in his thoughts. He needed to be on his A game to fly. "Grab the gas can. I'll check the engine. You check the exterior."

Victor surveyed the biplane, tugged on the cables, checked the wheels, and ran his hand over the wings. "Everything's solid and tight."

He handed Victor the gas can. "Put this under the shed and help me push her to the runway."

They pushed the Curtiss JN-Four so it headed into the wind. He tugged the hat over his thick hair and pulled the goggles over his eyes. "I'll get in, you prop her off."

Victor pulled the propeller and jumped away from the plane. Frankie waved, and the biplane roared down the runway. He climbed to five thousand feet and leveled off. The wind on his face and the clicking of the cylinders in the engine attempted to soothe his frayed nerves.

He focused on the familiar scenery, smoke curled out of Walter's chimney and cows grazed in the pasture. From the air, everything appeared the same, but inside the airplane self-doubt invaded his mind and heart. He knew Audrey was too good to be true when he met her. She looked and acted like a movie star from Hollywood, why would she be attracted to him in the first place?

He flew several circles around Walter Andrews'

farm. Andrews Field consisted of forty acres Victor's Uncle Walter gave him to start an airport when he married Dottie Lester.

The Jenny responded to his commands. He practiced some S-turns, breathing into the turn as his instructor taught him years ago. The muscles of his hands relaxed on the stick. He flew away from the farm so his daredevil tricks wouldn't scare the animals or Walter's wife Delores.

He aimed the plane toward the lake, a few miles from the farm. He flew around the perimeter of the water. A fisherman stood at the edge holding his pole and waiting for a catfish to bite. He continued his S-turns starting at one end of the lake and stopping at the other end. He continued the turns until all he thought about was flying. He guided the Jenny through loops. He climbed higher and picked up speed enabling him to break into barrel rolls. Satisfied with how the biplane responded, he started his favorite maneuver for smoothness and coordination, the Cuban-Eight. Frankie started the loop, came down the back side and did a half-roll, and glided into another loop, again half-rolling on the back side before pulling out.

He took the airplane higher and headed to earth in a dive. The lake gleamed ready to absorb his misery. The rush of the wind pummeled him. He could crash into the lake and refuse to face the mess he'd made of his life, or he could pull out of the dive. He struggled with the decision.

At the last minute, he yanked the stick. The gold digger wasn't worth losing his life. The plane climbed upward heading to five thousand feet. He inhaled, filled his lungs, blew the air through his lips, and decided he didn't want to die. He flew through town and into the next county before turning around. The last twenty minutes of his flight he thought of nothing but the sky.

The sound of the engine, the wind rocking the wings, the open sky, the sun on his face, the whining wires…ahh. His siren song. He started his descent. Al waved from the pasture. *Al, man he hated to disappoint the old man.* He landed the plane making a perfect three-point landing. The old man ran toward the biplane. He helped get her into the shed. "How was your flight?"

"Good." He appreciated his friend and his concern.

"Did it clear your head?" Al placed the chocks under each wheel.

Frankie threw the tarp over the seat openings. "Yeah, but didn't change anything. I'm still a fool."

"Don't let this worm spoil the apple. Cut it out and go on with yourself." Al helped him secure the tarp.

He gave a yank on the rope to make sure it was tight. "Thanks for the advice. I'm better off without the likes of her."

"Yes, you are, son." The old man walked beside him as they made their way to the hangar where Frankie began work on a Taylor Cub.

Al cleaned the bathroom and hung the mop on a nail to dry. "Boss is gone, he said to tell you to lock up when you leave. I'm gonna sweep, then I'm leavin'. See ya tomorrow."

He worked on the small plane until he had the engine repaired and tuned up. He would perform a test flight in the morning. He cranked his car and drove toward home.

The coupe, a piece of junk he found rusting away

in a farmer's pasture, shined like new money after his extensive repairs, new paint job, and lots of elbow grease. He lived like a rich man with a shiny car and house in town.

He liked his previous residence in the shanty town, and the people were his friends, but he preferred the luxuries of indoor plumbing and electricity. Audrey would've never lived in the squalor. She refused to go with him to visit his friends. He made the biggest mistake of his life and let her beauty cloud his judgment, but he missed her. In the two short months they were married, he raced home from work every day, eager to spend all his free time with his bride.

****

Frankie tossed until sleep found him. He woke early and extended his arm searching for Audrey. He opened his eyes, and the light from the moon cast a shadow in the bed. He swung his legs to the side and sat with his head in his hands, his mind recalled the events of yesterday. He stepped into his trousers and headed to the kitchen to make coffee. He craved his work and the familiarity of the hangar. His pulse beat faster when he remembered the Taylor Cub, he'd have the opportunity to test fly before the customer picked it up.

He parked beside Al's old blue Chevrolet truck. He walked into the hangar, tugged his leather jacket off, and hung it on a nail. "Morning, Al, where are you?"

Al shuffled from the bathroom with a mop and bucket in his hand. "Good morning, coffee's on the hot plate. Help yourself."

Frankie poured a cup of hot brew and placed two chairs next to each other. "Have a seat."

The janitor and all around handyman poured coffee

into a thick ceramic cup. He sat in the chair beside Frankie. "How you doin' this mornin', son?"

He never tired of Al calling him son. He hadn't seen his daddy since the day his mama died, eleven years ago. His old man left town before the last shovel of dirt got heaped on the mound. "I didn't sleep much last night. Still in shock. I can't believe anyone would do what she did."

Al drank a sip of coffee, stretched his legs, and crossed his ankles. "I never figured Miss Audrey was the one for you. Oh, she was pretty enough, but her heart wasn't in it. The way I see it, you got out easy. The mistake would have been if you were hitched, had a couple of kids, and then discovered the real Audrey. You'd be going through a divorce, broken home, and children you'd never see again. I think you need to count your blessings this little bird flew away."

Frankie drained his cup, set it on the table, and stood. "I know everything you said is true, it's not easy to forget or forgive. I don't know if I'll ever be able to trust another woman."

"You'll commit to the right one, and you'll know when she's right."

He stared at Al. He didn't think he would ever have faith in anyone again, man or woman. "I'm gonna get the Cub ready for a test flight."

The Taylor E-2 Cub had an open cockpit. He grabbed his jacket, hat, and goggles. The plane weighed less and was easier to handle than his biplane. The Cub had a single wing mounted high on the fuselage where the Jenny had double wings and a large engine in front.

He searched the hangar for his friend. "Can you prop me off?"

7

"Sure can."

They guided the plane to the runway. He climbed into the seat, put on his hat and goggles, and readied the engine, "Contact."

"Contact," Al yelled, and spun the propeller.

The engine fired. He taxied to the runway. He listened for any misfiring or roughness from the engine. Everything sounded right. The plane lifted off the ground. He kept the Cub in the air for fifteen minutes before he returned to Andrews Field.

The boss man's car turned into the parking lot as he landed the plane. He taxied close to the hanger. Victor and Al pushed the plane the rest of the way. Al chocked the wheels. He climbed from the plane and took a deep breath until his lungs were filled with air. He exhaled and gazed toward the sky hoping to keep the peaceful feeling he experienced when he soared through the air.

Victor stood inside the door. "How'd she run? Any problems?"

He removed his hat and goggles and placed them on his desk. "No, she purrs like a kitten. You might want to take her up. She's light as a feather and flies real smooth."

"You doin' better today?"

"Yeah, I'd like to say I've been through worse, but I can't." He opened the drawer to his desk and pulled out his to-do list.

"You better be glad you got rid of her this easy."

"Exactly what Al said. He mentioned something about a bird."

Victor laughed and shook his head. "What would we do without his words of wisdom? By the way,

Dottie and I are having a little party for Ruth Ann Saturday. This is her first weekend home since she started school. I want you to come. I think it'd do you good."

"I'll think about it." He grabbed a pencil and scratched through 'test fly Taylor Cub.'

"No one's going to say anything about Audrey, don't worry," his boss said, as he walked through the hanger to his office.

He wanted to go. Victor's family was all he had. They wouldn't say anything or judge him, anyone except Ruthie. Given the chance, she'd rub salt in his wound, twist it in deep, and he'd feel the grit the rest of his life. She wouldn't say anything with her family around, so he would avoid one on one contact with her...for a long time.

Chapter Two

A lone spotlight illuminated the middle of the stage. Ruth Ann Douglas' desire to act excited and scared her at the same time. She stood close enough to the light as to cast a soft glow on her monologue book. She searched for difficult lines, practicing them in a soft voice. Her hands trembled. The book hit the floor with a thud. She tiptoed to center stage, closed her eyes, and mentally crossed the threshold. She stared into the darkness and became Angellica, a courtesan of the 1600s. She and the universe were one. Her nerves were gone, calm coursed through her veins. She relished this moment in time and didn't want it to end, praying she would do the same at the audition.

Ronald Waters sat in his chair staring.

She tiptoed to the edge of the stage. "Well?"

His slow loud clapping filled the empty auditorium. "Do as well at your audition, and you'll get any part you want."

She put her hand over her eyes so she could see into the theater. "Thank you. It felt good. I remembered all my lines."

"You could give any actor in New York a run for their money." He walked toward the stage.

She laughed off the compliment. "Let's get to work on dialog in case we get our parts."

She met the young actor in September and

considered him one of her best friends. He danced and sang his way into the hearts of their classmates. He made sure everyone knew he wanted to perform on stage in New York. If anyone in the class could, it would be Ronald.

They worked for several hours until they were too hungry to go on.

He gathered his books. "Let me buy you supper."

"Thank you." She put on her coat and followed him out the door.

They arrived at the diner on the corner and ordered hamburgers, fries, and colas. While they waited on their food, they studied the script and recited lines.

"We've almost memorized all the lines." She put her notebook on the table.

He studied her face. "Memorizing the lines is the first step, but there's more."

She placed her hands on the table and leaned toward Ronald. "Mrs. James told me I'm too intelligent to be an actress."

"She did not." He gave her a disbelieving frown.

She raised her right hand as if swearing an oath. "She did. I asked her what she meant. She said I analyzed everything I did, and that I tried too hard."

"Yes, you do, but did she also say you're a very talented actress?" He reached for her hands cradling them in his.

She didn't expect the intimacy. A reflex tempted her to pull away. She looked into his green eyes, heat ran through her body.

He winked, giving her a devilish grin. "Go on. What'd she say next?"

"She advised me to use the threshold technique to

make an imaginary boundary between the everyday life and the creative world. She told me to cross into the magical world where my artist and spiritual energies could be liberated."

"You crossed the boundary tonight, I saw you. What else helps?"

She grabbed a salt shaker. "Using props helps me most of all because I can transfer my thoughts to an object."

"You're getting the idea." He took the shaker from her.

"In the monologue I have no props." She placed her hands palm up on the table.

He cradled her hands in his. "Something worked for you. I haven't seen anyone come close to what you did today."

She tugged her hands from his grasp as the waitress set their plates in front of them. "I have the best coach. Thanks for helping me. Everyone knows you're the best in the class."

He grinned before he took a bite of his hamburger.

She dipped a fry in ketchup. "Why are you staring at me?"

Ronald swallowed. He grabbed a napkin from the holder to wipe his mouth. "Whether we do or we don't get these parts, I've enjoyed playing your love interest." He locked his eyes with hers.

Heat rose in her belly. She fidgeted and dropped her eyes to her burger. She sipped cola through the straw as she watched him dig into his supper. She liked him as a friend. She hadn't thought of him as a boyfriend. He was handsome but not as tall as she liked. He had a dancer's lean body punctuated by a short hair style. His skin appeared as smooth as hers. She was certain she smelled Pond's Extract Vanishing Cream on his face when they were practicing one of their scenes. His peculiar ways had to be a by-product of his profession. Dating a man who understood her dreams captivated her. "Sure, I'd like to see more of you, too."

The food was gone except for a lone french fry on Ruth Ann's plate. Ronald ate the fry, wiped his hands, and grabbed the bill. "You ready to go?" He stood and reached for her hand.

The night air blasted her exposed hands and face. They huddled close as they strolled along the sidewalk. He guided her to a bench and brushed the leaves from the seat. "Let's sit and rest a few minutes."

She gazed at the full moon, shining like a street light. "I've always loved the night sky. You should see the heavens from my uncle's farm. On a clear night when you're out in the pasture with no trees around, you can see every star in the sky."

He followed her gaze. "You sound homesick."

"I am, a little. I wanted to live in the city, now not so sure."

"When I graduate, I'll move to New York. I've dreamed of working in New York since I attended a Broadway show with my parents when I was ten. I hope you feel the same. We could go together." He regarded her and watched for a reaction.

She stared into the night and imagined New York with people milling around under the blinking lights of the city. "I get inspired to live in New York when I read my Theatre Arts Magazines. After living in Atlanta, I just want to go back to Saplingville to start my own theater."

He shifted her face toward him. "Right now, I want to be wherever you are."

Ruth Ann searched his eyes. She knew he wanted to kiss her. He didn't disappoint. Ronald moaned as his kiss deepened. His hand found its way inside her coat. One thing about a big city, she didn't have to worry about anyone she knew seeing her neck with a young man. She enjoyed kissing and had the reputation of a tease. Leaves rustled. Someone headed their way. She tugged his hand from under her coat. "I think we should go home. We have an early day tomorrow."

"Sure thing, let's go." He put his arm around her and guided her toward her living quarters.

She wasn't sure if she liked him, or she craved warmth in the cold night air. He surprised her. A romance with him never entered her mind.

They approached her apartment. She gave him her full attention. "Thanks, Ronald, for a lovely night."

He placed a good night kiss on her lips. "I had a great time, too. See you tomorrow."

She hung her coat on the peg by the door. She walked to the middle of her residence to let the warmth of the floor heater take away the chill. She basked in the warmth and leaned against the wall with her eyes closed. *The most popular guy in class likes me.*

Her body tingled with excitement. She did a ballet pirouette into her bedroom. With Ronald she forgot about her homesickness. *I hope he can help me forget about Frankie marrying the damn gold digger.*

Chapter Three

Ruth Ann's taxi snaked through the crowded parking lot of Candler Field. She stepped from the car, focusing her gaze on the small planes. Her brother stood next to his airplane, waving. She said a silent prayer, thanking God he flew the bright yellow airplane instead of the biplane. She liked an airplane with cabin windows. Flying in the open cockpit of the Jenny scared her.

Victor walked toward the taxi. He paid the driver before taking her suitcase.

She hugged her brother. "Thanks for taking me home."

"No problem. How's school?"

"Great, I had my audition yesterday. I hope I get the part."

"When will ya know?" He guided her toward the Cessna.

"They'll post the lineup next week." She watched a large airplane lift off into the air. "That's a big plane."

Victor gazed at the Stinson Tri-Motor. "Yep, three motors in the front." He turned his attention back to his sister. "Good luck. I'm sure you did fine in your audition."

"I did my best. I've got a friend who helped me go over my lines."

He smiled studying her face. "Does this friend have

a name?"

"Yes, his name is Ronald." Heat flowed to her cheeks.

"Oh, Ronald, huh?" He teased. "I assume he's an actor?"

"He's the best in the class. He plans to go to New York after graduation." She skipped toward the airplane.

"What are your plans when you graduate?" He threw the suitcase behind her seat and took her hand as she climbed in the airplane.

"Still trying to decide. How's everyone at home?"

He crossed to the other side of the plane giving the exterior a once-over before climbing into his seat. He fastened his seatbelt and studied the check list. "We had some excitement last week."

"Give me the scoop." She pulled her seatbelt tighter.

She watched her brother ready the plane for take-off. She'd worshiped him since she was a little girl. He joined the United States Army Air Corps and to her delight, returned to Saplingville, met Dottie, and got married. He started his airport business instead of flying for a commercial airline.

The plane leveled off. She took a deep breath, her ridged muscles relaxed against the seat. Over the roar of the engine, she raised her voice. "Okay, tell me what happened."

He glanced at the airplane gauges. "I'll tell you; however, I don't want you rubbing it in Frankie's face. He feels bad enough already."

Her heart sunk in her chest. "Frankie...what are you talking about, what happened? Is he hurt?"

He chuckled. "No, although, it'd be easier for him to get over a black eye from a brawl than it will to get over this."

She put her hand on the dashboard of the airplane and stared.

"He found out Audrey was already married when they got married in September." Victor spoke over the roar of the engine.

"Who was she married to?"

"A man named Charles Wallace. Searched for her since May. Even hired a gumshoe."

She sighed and closed her eyes. "Poor Frankie."

He faced his sister. "Ruth Ann, look at me."

She stared at the floor of the plane. She remembered the time he threw her cigarettes out the car window and threatened to tell their mother. She gazed at her brother waiting for his reprimand.

"Ruth Ann, please, please don't harass him. I know this is just the sort of thing you would love to needle him about. Don't. He feels bad enough."

A calmness flooded through her she hadn't felt since she learned he married Audrey. *Frankie isn't married.*

Realization of what she'd done caused guilt to replace the calmness. She didn't want Frankie to get married. She liked the attention he lavished on her. She ignored him and treated him like a jerk, so he found someone else. She blamed herself for his marriage to the gold digger. "So I guess Audrey left with her husband. I mean the man she was legally married to."

"Yes, thank God she's gone. Promise me you'll be nice." Victor checked his gauges.

"I promise. Will he be at Andrews Field when we

land?"

"Probably. He's keeping to himself so he may not be talkative."

She thought about the handsome man. She ignored his advances, laughed, and called him terrible names to his face. Secretly, she longed for the attention he gave her until Audrey arrived in town and caught his eye.

Everyone recognized him as a tough guy, but she knew the real Frankie. He'd give you the shirt off his back if you asked. "So they aren't married?"

"No, we talked to a lawyer to make sure. He assured us the marriage wasn't legal since Audrey was married when they said their vows."

"What's he so upset about? Did he love her that much?" The thought of Frankie loving anyone but her brought the jealous thoughts she'd tamped down to the surface. She glanced out the window as the earth drew closer.

Victor started his descent toward Andrews Field. "No, I don't think he ever loved her. My guess is, she asked him to marry her. He's upset because she made a fool of him."

"Ridiculous. He's not a fool." She closed her eyes and silently prayed they'd land safely.

"We've all told him. Do not mention this, you hear me?" He surveyed the instruments and concentrated on the landing.

She clenched her seat as the plane descended. "I won't say anything. I promise." The airplane touched the ground. She opened her eyes, released the air she held in her lungs, and let her body relax against the seat. She appreciated her brother's smooth landing.

He taxied toward the hangar.

When the propeller stopped, she opened the door and jumped from the plane eager to see Frankie. She ran in the hangar surveying the surroundings. His car stood in the parking lot, and his leather jacket hung on a nail.

Al stood at a table near the door sorting tools. She wandered over. "Hi, Mr. Gregory. How are you?"

"Fine, and you?"

"Swell." She hesitated, searching the hangar. "Is Frankie around?"

Light shown from the old man's eyes while a huge grin filled his face. "He was here a few minutes ago. I don't know where he got off to. How you doin' at actin' school?"

"Good, I like it." She wouldn't get anything out of Al. If Frankie was hiding from her, he was in on it.

"And Atlanta, you like the big city?"

She gazed through the glass window into Victor's office. "I like it fine."

Her brother stuck his head in the door. "Ready to go see Ma and Pa?"

She gazed through the hangar one more time, hoping to see Frankie appear from one of the rooms. "Yeah, I'm ready. See you Mr. Gregory."

She climbed into Victor's car. She watched the airport fade out of sight. *Damn it, I need to see Frankie. I'll see him before I go back to school, if I have to go to his house.*

****

Frankie opened the supply room door.

Al continued to put the tools in order. "You can come out now. She's gone."

He wandered into the hangar. "I've stooped to

hiding. What an idiot."

"You ain't no idiot. She wanted to see you. If you'd seen the disappointment in her face when you were nowhere to be found, you'd have run out to meet her."

"Ruthie and I have a long history of harassing each other. She wanted to rub in the mistake I made with Audrey." He grabbed a wrench and placed it with the others.

"Needling and fussing is how you and Miss Prissy communicate, since neither of you will admit how much you like each other. I see how you watch her like a dog cravin' a bone. She puts on a highfalutin air to ignore you. What you don't see is her watchin' you with a dreamy glint in her eye."

Frankie said, "I don't see it."

Al smiled and counted screw drivers. "Course you don't."

He gathered tools from his work station and placed them on the table. They worked together in silence. The last time he saw Ruthie, he was with Audrey. They were gathered at Victor's house for supper. When he made eye contact with her, she glanced away. She ate and left without a word. He figured she was mad because it was one of the few times she didn't have one of the Saplingville boys hanging on her arm. When she left for school, he married Audrey.

Al guided the table with rollers to the side wall. "I heard Victor ask you to supper Saturday. Ya need to go. Check out what she's been up to. I bet she's homesick for more than her family."

"What? Give her the chance to harass me about my foolishness? No thanks." He grabbed his leather jacket.

"Think about it, son. You need to be with people who love you right now." He put on his hat and denim jacket.

They stepped outside, and Frankie locked the door.

Al opened the door to his truck. "You have fun this weekend. I'll see you Monday morning bright and early."

"Thanks. Tell Ethel hello."

Frankie drove by Joe's Tavern on his way home. He parked, silenced the engine, and watched people come and go. A young couple arrived in a new car. The man opened the door for his date and kissed her. He started his car and backed out of the parking space. Being around people wasn't going to dispel his loneliness; he'd rather be alone in his own home.

Chapter Four

Ruth Ann ran in the house while Victor collected her suitcase. "Ma, I'm home."

Hattie rushed from the kitchen, wiping her hands on her apron. "Ruth Ann, I've missed you so." She embraced her daughter. "I'm glad you're home."

She hugged her mother and followed her to the kitchen. The familiar smell of lemon cleanser along with Ma standing at the counter organizing the utensils she needed for biscuits elevated her homesickness to another level. She opened the lid of the pot on the stove. The aroma of beef stew hit her in the face. "This smells delicious."

"I put it on early this morning. The meat should be good and tender. How's school?" Hattie handed her a glass of water.

"School's great. I auditioned for a part in a play. They'll post assignments next week."

She sat on the brown soda fountain stool in the corner of the kitchen. Her father salvaged it when he got new ones for the drug store he opened in 1905. Jacob had a heart attack two years ago and sold part of Douglas Drug Store to Ned Ayers, a young pharmacist. They ran the store together.

Hattie had her right hand in the biscuit dough using her left hand to pour milk into the mixture. "Sounds wonderful. I'm sure you'll get the part. What's the name of the play?"

"*The Three Sisters* by Anton Chekhov. He was a Russian playwright." She twirled around on the stool.

Hattie shuffled to the sink to wash her hands before she rolled the dough into biscuits. "Russian, you mean you have to do a play in Russian?"

"No, Ma. The play's in English. The man who wrote it's from Russia. He's dead now. His plays are performed all over the world."

She dried her hands and tucked the towel in the drawer pull. "I'm so proud of you. You're learning more than I ever thought possible." She placed the biscuits in the pan. "Have you met any nice boys?"

She didn't want to tell her mother too much about Ronald. Hattie wanted her to get married and settle down. She chose her words. "There's a boy named Ronald. He's the best actor in our class. We run lines and rehearse together."

She opened the oven door and deposited the biscuits on the rack. "I'd like to meet this Ronald. He sounds very nice."

The back door opened. Lisbeth strolled into the kitchen. "Hey, sis, welcome home. How's life in Atlanta?"

She glared at her sister. With a two year age difference, they should be closer. They didn't fight like most sisters. They tolerated each other. Lisbeth played the piano at church, never bragged, or demanded attention, the perfect studious daughter. Trouble found Ruth Ann, whether she looked for it or not. She and Hattie locked horns all through her high school years. "I'm having the time of my life."

"Good. I wouldn't expect you to have anything

less."

Ruth Ann crossed her arms. "What about you? What are your plans when you graduate? Law school or medical school?" She locked eyes with her sister and picked up a secret vibe. She was holding something back.

"Neither, I haven't decided yet." Lisbeth opened the lid on the pot of beef stew, picked up the spoon, and stirred.

Hattie said, "I don't understand you girls. Why do you have to go to school? What's wrong with finding a nice young man so you can get married? I want you to live close to me so I can enjoy my grandchildren."

She didn't want to hear her mother's lecture. "Lisbeth, I'm going upstairs to unpack. Come with me. I might need some help."

Lisbeth sat in the barrel back chair next to the bed watching her sister. "So, how is it? Must be exciting to live in a big city."

Ruth Ann closed the bedroom door. She sat on her bed trying to decide how much to tell. "Lonely most of the time. We work all day, running lines and rehearsing. Memorizing takes most of my time. I'm learning technique, diction, how to be funny, when to be serious. The time spent away from class is always with other students. I rehearse with people trying for the same part I am. It's intimidating to say the least."

"Have you met any boys?" Lisbeth twirled her hair around her finger.

She lowered her voice. "Don't tell Ma, you know how she gets her hopes up. I'm dating a boy named Ronald. I like him. He kisses good."

"Make sure all you do is kiss. You got away with

leading the boys from here on. Atlanta's not Saplingville." Lisbeth leaned in the chair and crossed her arms.

"Don't worry. I can take care of myself. What do you know about Frankie and Audrey?"

Lisbeth shook her head, "I feel sorry for him. He's a nice man, but trouble seems to follow him wherever he goes. We haven't seen him since she left. Victor told us she was married to another man, so their marriage wasn't legal. He said Frankie didn't take it well. He's embarrassed. I think he should be glad she's gone. Nothing but trouble, that one."

She placed her suitcase under the bed. "I'm glad she's gone, too. So tell me, I know you've decided what you want to do after you finish school. Let's hear it."

"I won't tell Ma about Ronald if you don't say anything about my plans. I'll tell them when I'm ready."

She climbed to the middle of her bed and sat with her legs crossed under her. "Deal, spill the beans."

"I want to be an airplane pilot, like Victor." She gave her sister a smug grin.

Ruth Ann's mouth dropped open. "An airplane pilot? Why? I mean, I don't mind riding in the plane. I sure don't want to fly the thing. How many women fly airplanes anyway?"

"You've heard of Amelia Earhart, haven't you?" Lisbeth rolled her eyes and stared at the ceiling.

"Of course, I have, dummy. She's an exception."

Lisbeth stood and stared out the window. "No, you're wrong. There're lots of women pilots. Some are better than Victor and Frankie. Remember when Louise Thaden won the Women's Air Derby in 1929?"

She calculated the numbers in her head. "Wait, you were nine years old then."

Lisbeth gazed at the heavens. "Victor was in the United States Army Air Corps learning to fly bombers. I decided if Victor could fly, I could too." She turned toward her sister. "I heard the news about the race on the radio. Last year I did research for a report. Found out there were nineteen female pilots flying from Santa Monica, California, to Cleveland, Ohio. They faced many obstacles. Some airplanes were sabotaged by jealous men. They continued on with fifteen completing the race. If these women can fly, I can too."

She shook her head in disbelief. "Boy, Pa was upset when I told him I wanted to be an actress. I can't wait to hear what he says about your plans."

Lisbeth sat on the bed next to her sister. "You promised not to tell. I'll tell them when I'm ready."

"Make sure I'm home. I wouldn't miss this for the world."

"Did Ma tell you Victor and Dottie are having a party for you at their house tomorrow?" Lisbeth stood to leave.

"No, she didn't mention it. Who's coming?"

"Mostly family."

"Sounds like fun, I'll be down in a few minutes." She hoped Frankie would join them. She had to see him. So much had happened to both of them in the last two months. She heard Hattie's call to supper. She had lots of stuff to tell them about school, leaving out the part about necking on a park bench with a boy.

Chapter Five

Ruth Ann, Lisbeth, Jacob, and Hattie arrived early to the party so Hattie could help Dottie with the food. Ruth Ann took the deviled eggs from her mother handing them to Lisbeth.

She held out her hands. "I'll take the congealed salad."

Her mother refused. "No, I'll take this, it might slide off the plate."

She ran to the front porch taking the seat on the swing next to Dottie. She kissed Carol Ann and Jack Andrew on the forehead. Both babies wanted her. She took them from Dottie, holding both became a challenge. Carol Ann tangled her hands in her hair, and Jack Andrew dove straight for her earbob.

Dottie reached for her little boy. "One at a time. They're eight months old now. They won't be still."

She sat the baby girl in her lap facing her. "They'll be walking soon. You're going to have your hands full."

Jack Andrew squirmed wanting to climb in her lap.

Jacob wrestled his grandson from Dottie. He lifted him over his head. "How's my big boy doing?"

Dottie smiled at her father-in-law. "Thanks, Pa. He's getting so strong, I can hardly hold him when he wants something."

Jacob settled the baby on his hip. "Head strong.

Stubborn. Just like his daddy."

Ruth Ann spotted Uncle Walter and Aunt Delores pull in front of the house in their old Ford truck. Her uncle used it for all his farming chores. The wooden boards on the bed of the truck were scratched, but the old truck still looked good. She passed Carol Ann to Dottie and ran down the steps into the yard.

She opened the door for Delores. Her aunt enveloped her in a big hug. "How's my little Ruth Ann? We've missed you."

Walter made his way around the truck. "We're so proud of you, going off to the big city by yourself." He lifted the crate of food holding it so nothing would spill.

Delores linked her arm through Ruth Ann's. "I think my husband's a little jealous. He's only been to Atlanta twice in his life."

"I'm homesick." She walked close to her aunt breathing in the scent of the lilac perfume the old lady always wore.

Delores smiled at her niece. "I hope you're making friends."

"I spend at least ten hours a day with my classmates." She didn't consider all of them friends. "I like most of them."

Her aunt pulled her closer. "Sounds like a lot of work. Do you like it?"

"I love the work." She heard a car door close and watched Dottie's daddy, Avery and his wife Annie exit a shiny new car. "You go in. I'll say hello to Mr. and Mrs. Lester."

She skipped toward the street. "I'm glad you could make it. Nice car."

Avery ran his hand over the hood. "Nineteen thirty-five Plymouth. Arrived yesterday. The boss let me drive it for the weekend. He thinks the more I know about the cars, the easier for me to sell 'em."

"Welcome home, Ruth Ann." Annie gave the pound cake to Avery.

Avery escorted the two ladies. "How's school?"

"Fine. I auditioned for a play this week."

"Good luck. Hope you get the part." Avery stepped back and let the women climb the stairs to the porch.

She held the front door open for the Lesters while she gazed into the house. Lisbeth sat on a blanket playing with the twins. Her brother stood at the kitchen counter slicing a baked chicken. She eased to the kitchen. "Victor, thanks for having this party for me. I've missed y'all. Is everyone here?"

He separated a drum stick from a thigh. "I invited Frankie. I don't know if he's coming. He likes a party, if for nothing else but the food. I reminded him yesterday."

She set out glasses and filled them with ice for the tea. "I'd like to see him."

He put the knife on the counter and stared at his sister. "Be nice, okay?"

"I'll be nice if he is."

He picked up the knife and continued to carve. "Neither of you can be nice to each other. Don't mention Audrey."

She poured tea in glasses. "I won't."

Everyone held hands while Jacob blessed the food and thanked God for their many blessings.

As soon as he said 'Amen,' Dottie cleared the way. "Guest of honor first."

Ruth Ann grabbed a plate. She milled around the

kitchen counter getting a little bit of everything. A knock on the door caused her stomach to churn.

Victor greeted his guest, "Frankie, glad you could make it, man."

A grin bloomed on her face. She stood in the kitchen door and watched.

Frankie patted Victor on the back. "Thanks for inviting me." He grabbed Jack Andrew, lifted him over his head and guided him through the air like an airplane. The baby laughed while his twin crawled to him and used Frankie's leg to stand. He scooped Carol Ann, holding one child in each arm. They both pounced on his face. He shook his head and blew air threw his lips. Both babies mimicked him.

She took her plate to the parlor, sat on the couch, and hoped Frankie would join her.

Victor reached for Carol Ann and cradled her in his arms. "Let's put them in their high chairs so we can fix our plate."

Frankie placed Jack Andrew in his seat. "The food smells good. The women in your family are the best cooks in the world."

He joined Jacob in line. "Evening, Mr. Douglas."

"Frankie, glad you could join us to welcome my daughter home." Jacob placed a piece of chicken on his plate.

"I'm proud you asked me. How are you feeling?" He took a plate from the stack.

"I'm better than ever. Ned's a great help at the drug store. He runs the store like I do, couldn't have found a better partner." Jacob spooned a small amount of every vegetable on his plate.

"I hope Victor feels the same about me at the

airfield." He filled his plate with food and topped it off with a biscuit and piece of cornbread.

"Victor couldn't have found a better person to help him run Andrews Field."

"Thank you, sir." He walked to the kitchen table where Walter sat alone. "Mind if I join you?"

Walter scooted his chair over to give Frankie plenty of room. "Not at all. I saw you flying the Jenny last week. A very impressive Cuban Eight."

He grabbed a glass of iced tea off the counter. "I hoped I was far enough away from the farm. I didn't disturb anything, did I?"

"No, I was repairing the fence by the lake and saw the show. Impressive. I haven't seen those aerobatics since your time with the flying circus."

Frankie put his fork on his plate. "I needed to clear my head. Flying the Jenny's like medicine to me."

Walter stood at the dessert table surveying the pickin's. "You shouldn't give the matter anymore thought, none of us are. We're your friends, Frankie. We're here for you."

"Thanks, Mr. Andrews." He ate his food and rubbed his last bite of bread on the plate to sop the bean juice. He poured a cup of coffee to drink with his pound cake and made his way to the parlor. He placed his cup on a table and stood to eat his dessert.

Lisbeth patted the seat next to her. "Frankie, sit with me."

He grabbed his cup placing it on the coffee table before he sat. "Lisbeth, how are you?"

Lisbeth surveyed the room. She lowered her voice. "I need to talk to you about something. Confidentially."

He sipped his coffee. "I'm listening."

She put her hand over her mouth and whispered, "I want you to teach me how to fly."

Frankie set his plate on the table. He turned to give her his full attention. "I see. What do your parents say about this? I remember your father wasn't happy about Victor's choice of profession."

"They don't know…yet."

"Don't you think we should get their permission first?"

Lisbeth clasped her hands. "I guess."

"I'll talk to Victor. You talk to Mr. and Mrs. Douglas. I'll do all I can to help you, if that's what you want to do."

Lisbeth smiled a toothy grin. "Thank you. I knew I could depend on you."

Ruth Ann watched her sister talk to Frankie. *What are they talking about?* The conversation appeared serious until Lisbeth smiled like a Cheshire Cat. *What's going on?*

She'd find out before she left to go to school tomorrow. Frankie avoided her which gave her the opportunity to admire the handsome, rugged, fit, and rough around the edges man. She liked his red hair and freckles and his towering presence. She compared him to Ronald, total opposites, but Ronald liked her so she would keep her options open. She didn't think Frankie would be out searching for another wife any time soon.

****

Ruth Ann put on her pajamas and walked down the hall to Lisbeth's bedroom determined to find out about the conversation with Frankie. Lisbeth sat at her desk writing a letter.

She sat in a chair waiting for her to finish her

scribbling. "What did you talk to Frankie about?"

Lisbeth folded the letter and slid it in an envelope. "Jealous?"

"No, I'm not jealous."

"I watched you chase him around the house. You put on quite a show." She opened the drawer, found a stamp, and licked it.

"That obvious?"

"Yes." She placed the stamp on the envelope.

"I must have looked stupid."

Lisbeth faced her sister. "You did."

"What were you talking about?"

Lisbeth gave Ruth Ann a huge smile. "I asked him to give me flying lessons."

"Why'd you ask Frankie? I would think Victor would be your first choice...he is your brother."

"Of course, I want Victor to teach me. He's military trained and does everything by the book."

Ruth Ann sat on the bed. "Yet, you're talking to Frankie, not Victor."

"Frankie learned from barnstormers who fly by their gut instinct. It's like playing the piano. People who play by ear put their heart into their playing. Pianists who rely on music often sound stilted because they're thinking too much about technique to let the music flow from their heart. I learned to play by ear, listening to Ma, then I started lessons. I add the music I hear in my head with the music on the page to create my own sound." She stood and twirled around with her arms spread. "I want it all, the technical and book knowledge combined with the instinct of a stunt pilot." She sat on the bed beside her sister.

"I understand, my acting coach says I think too

much. Acting isn't so much about intelligence as getting your intelligence out of the way to enable the creative side of your brain to take over. I can see where instinct would help with technical knowledge in flying an airplane." She stood gazing down at her sister. "Good luck, if it's what you want to do with your life."

"I want this more than anything. Nothing's going to stop me." Lisbeth stood and turned the cover down on her bed.

She tiptoed to her bedroom. Everything and everyone had changed. Lisbeth wanted to be a pilot. Frankie married a woman who was already married, and Ruth Ann realized her plan of moving to New York wasn't what she wanted.

Chapter Six

Frankie ground coffee beans for his morning pot of strong coffee. Closing his eyes and breathing in the smell, he remembered his mother's kitchen. He added an extra scoop to the basket like she taught him. The water bubbling in the knob of the percolator transfixed him. He stared into the glass ball and saw Ruthie's face. He shook it off and poured a cup of coffee.

He placed several strips of bacon in an iron skillet and sipped his coffee while the meat sizzled. Taking fresh butter Delores made, he slathered a slice of bread and slid the pan in the oven. Next, he cracked an egg into the hot bacon grease, letting the egg cook on one side before flipping to make his egg over easy.

Going to church flitted through his mind. He and Audrey didn't attend church. She wanted to stay home on Sundays or fly in his plane. She didn't like to be around people, now he understood why. He planned to get into the routine of church, but today wasn't the day. Ruthie would be at church with her family. Last night he avoided her, arrived late to the party, and hung with the guys, except for Lisbeth. Mr. and Mrs. Douglas were going to be shocked when they learned she wanted to take flying lessons. He didn't know any female pilots, but Lisbeth would succeed at anything she did.

He drank a second cup of coffee while he washed

dishes. A knock at this early hour surprised him. He peaked out the window before opening the door. "Victor, come in. What's going on? Why aren't you at church?"

"I would be, but I got a call from a client. They want me to take them to Macon today. I need you to fly Ruth Ann to Atlanta. You can take the Beechcraft Staggerwing."

His stomach knotted, and his breakfast churned. He swallowed willing his food to stay where it was. "Why can't I fly the client to Macon and you take Ruthie?"

"They asked for me. What's wrong? You always jump at the chance to fly the Beechcraft." Victor stared at him.

He didn't want to cause trouble with his job, his boss had enough stress. They had more work than both of them could do, but Victor couldn't afford another employee. The flight wouldn't take long, and then she'd be in Atlanta out of his hair. "You're the boss."

"Thanks, buddy. Pick her up at the house at two o'clock."

Frankie smiled and did a little bow. "Will do."

He stepped outside the door and watched Victor walk to his car. The sunshine brought warmth to his front porch. He stepped inside and grabbed a flannel shirt so he could enjoy the modest heat of the November day. He sat in his porch swing and read the Sunday paper.

His thoughts drifted to Ruthie. If she started any of her usual crap, he would tell her to mind her own business. It was time she outgrew her petty remarks and bitchy behavior. She infuriated him. When memories of her invaded his mind, he either fumed at her last scathing comments to him or his prick got hard and he had to take a cold shower. Even married to a woman like Audrey, his mind slipped to Ruthie every day. How could one woman control his emotions like she did? Was she a witch? He sat staring into the blue sky thinking first about Ruthie, then about Audrey. He contemplated becoming a monk. As much as he liked to pray and read his bible, he didn't want to do it all the time. He also didn't want to shave his head. *Me, living in a monastery. What a joke.*

He glanced at his pocket watch. Time to get ready. The faster he got Her Highness to Atlanta, the better.

Chapter Seven

Ruth Ann placed her suitcase by the front door. She stood at the window, watching for her brother's car. The Ford coupe barreled up the driveway. Frankie stepped out and walked toward the house. A smile filled her face, and her heart raced. *Is he coming to see me?* Hope bubbled in her heart. She opened the door as he stepped on the front porch.

He lowered his head. "I've come to take you to Atlanta. Victor had a job today. He asked me to fly you."

She would be alone with him in the plane until they arrived at Candler Field. She disguised her excitement. "Thank you for doing this. I appreciate it."

He shuffled his feet. "No problem, just doin' my job."

"Come in, I need to tell everyone goodbye." She raced to the parlor and hugged her parents.

He stood in the door and watched.

Lisbeth whispered, "Have fun, my sis got her wish. She's wanted to be alone with you since she got home."

"That's what I'm afraid of." His glance paused on Ruthie.

Hattie led her daughter to the door. "Frankie, you be careful."

"I will, Mrs. Douglas." They walked toward his car. He placed her suitcase behind the front seat. He bent and extended his hand. "Your chariot awaits."

She placed her hand on his as she got in the car. She settled in her seat and marveled at the interior. She remembered when Frankie bought the piece of junk. He'd worked hard to restore the 1930 Ford Model A Coupe. The tan car with black fenders and white sidewall tires was one of the best looking cars in town. She felt proud to ride in the fancy automobile. She realized how far he'd come by sheer determination and hard work. "Thank you for flying me. What plane are we taking?"

"The Staggerwing, otherwise, I'll have to take you in the Jenny."

She breathed a sigh of relief. She felt safer in the Staggerwing or the Cessna. "No, the red plane's fine."

"Red plane? You identify them by color?" He slowed the car and turned onto the main highway.

"I couldn't care less about the name of the plane, my concern is safety." She watched out the window as they left town and the land opened to pastures.

Frankie studied Ruthie's profile. "You look different. Your hair's shorter."

She fluffed her hair on the back of her head. "Easier for school. Sometimes, I need to wear a wig."

He licked his lips and stared at her long neck. "How do you like school?"

She faced him. Their eyes met and she felt a strange sensation in her belly. She gasped for air. After a long moment, she responded. "I love school, but I don't like Atlanta. The city's big and too many people. I wanted to go to New York after graduation. I've changed my mind."

"So you're going to return to Saplingville?" His

voice was almost a whisper.

"Maybe, but coming home feels weird. It doesn't seem like home anymore. So much has changed in the last few months." She watched Frankie slow the car and down shift to make the turn.

He wound the car into the large driveway at Andrews Field. "You've grown into a young lady. You're not a child anymore. You're gonna face lots of changes."

She sat in the car waiting for Frankie to open the door.

He opened it and made a bow. They strolled to the Beechcraft Staggerwing biplane. He placed her suitcase behind the seat and took her hand. He guided her in the airplane. She settled in her seat and fastened the seat belt tight around her waist.

She loved to watch him work. The handsome, strong, Frankie Howard. Known for his dare devil flying skills and drinking at Joe's Tavern. Most people didn't know what a kind, sweet, caring man he was.

He settled in the pilot seat. He started the engine adjusting controls until the propeller and engine sounded like he wanted, then headed to the runway.

She had questions but would wait until they were in the air. When he relaxed, she knew they were cruising toward Atlanta.

She drew in a deep breath and swallowed. She spoke loudly so he could hear her over the engine noise. "So, bad luck with Audrey, huh?"

"Yes. It was." He stared straight ahead.

"I can't believe anyone would do such a thing. Bigamy's a crime. She's a criminal. She didn't tell you she was married?"

He stared through the windshield. "If she told me she was married, I wouldn't have married her."

She narrowed her gaze. "Would you have dated her?"

"What kind of question is that? Of course I wouldn't date a married woman." His voice grew louder.

"Well, you did." She stared out the side window.

"Yes, I did. I didn't know she was married." He studied the instrument panel.

She swung her attention to his handsome face. "What did you see in her anyway?"

He leered at her. "Well, let's see. She was gorgeous, she was sexy, she was willing." He lowered his voice. "She said she loved me."

A fit of rage burned through her body. "I'll bet she didn't have blonde hair. Looked bleached to me. She wasn't beautiful, either. I think she had a big nose."

He turned toward her, their eyes locked together. After several seconds he found his voice. "Can we change the subject? I made a mistake. I want everyone to forget it so I can get on with my life."

She reined in her jealousy. "I'm sorry. I'm worried about you, is all."

Frankie scowled using his words to put her in her place. "No, you've always loved putting me down. This is the ultimate joke for you, isn't it?"

She wondered why they always argued. "No, I'm sorry about what happened. You deserve more than Audrey Gordon or whoever she is."

Noise from the engine filled the plane. She stared into the sky waiting for an answer.

He glanced her way. "Thanks."

The tension in the cockpit eased. She relaxed in her seat and stared at the blue sky. She glanced out of the window at the railroad tracks below them. Frankie and Victor used railroads and rivers as navigation aids. He veered the plane left, she watched the tracks disappear as they flew over a pine forest. The city loomed ahead with roads, buildings, and lots of cars. The airplane dropped in altitude, she spotted the airport.

He readied the plane for landing at Candler Field. "Are you taking a taxi?"

"No, one of my friends from school is meeting me. He's one of the few of us who have a car." She grabbed the sides of her seat.

"Does he have a name?" Frankie concentrated on the descent.

"Ronald Waters. He's from Montgomery, Alabama." She closed her eyes and prayed for a safe landing.

He landed the plane and guided it to a parking spot. "I'd like to meet your friend from Alabama."

She'd planned to jump out, get her suitcase, and get in Ronald's car. "You don't have to. I know you need to get home."

"No problem, I'll help you with your suitcase." He walked close with his hand on her back.

Ronald leaned against the hood of his car and waved. He hurried toward her with his arms open. She stepped aside. "Ronald, I'd like you to meet Frankie. He was kind enough to fly me to Atlanta today. Victor had to work."

Ronald stuck out his hand. "Nice to meet you. Thanks for taking care of my girl."

"Yeah, nice to meet you, too." Frankie gave his

hand a firm shake. He faced Ruthie. "Let us know if you need a ride home. One of us will come and get you."

She didn't want him to leave. She didn't know if it was because she wanted to be with him or if he was her lifeline home. "Thanks Frankie, have a safe flight."

Chapter Eight

Ronald drove through the streets of Atlanta chattering about his weekend. He and some classmates enjoyed a night at the picture show where *Top Hat* featuring his idol, Fred Astaire played to a packed audience. "Can't wait to show you the new dance steps I learned from the movie."

She didn't hear a word he said. Her thoughts were with the handsome barnstormer.

He raised his voice to get her attention. "Ruth Ann, I missed you this weekend. Did you miss me?"

She focused on Ronald. "I'm sorry. I must be tired from the flight. What'd you say?"

"I missed you." He reached for her hand.

"I missed you, too," she lied. If she had thought about Ronald, she would have missed him. "I appreciate the ride to school. They post the cast list tomorrow. I can't wait."

"Me either. I can't wait to be your on-stage boyfriend, too."

Ronald thinks I'm his girlfriend. "This should make our acting easier, huh?"

"Sure will." They arrived at her living quarters. He carried her suitcase. "Can I come in?"

"Of course, come in. I'll fix us a cola. Have a seat." She opened the refrigerator taking out two bottles and the ice tray from the freezer compartment.

Ronald crept to the kitchen. He spun her around to face him. "Mind if I do this?"

His kisses on her neck gave her goose bumps. He made his way to her lips. She melted into him, meeting his deep kisses with her own. Before she knew it, Ronald sat on the settee with her in his lap. She put her arms around his neck, her lips as greedy as his. His hand brushed her nipple, and she shook with desire. Her blouse tightened as he wrestled with the buttons. She removed his hand from her blouse, scooted out of his lap, and sat beside him. "Wow, where'd you learn to kiss?"

"It takes two to kiss." He lowered his head to claim another one. She stood and walked to the kitchen. "Let me get our drinks."

She hoped he wouldn't follow, she had to get a hold of her feelings. If her mother knew she necked with a boy alone in her apartment, she would be in big trouble. It would be so easy to give in. No one would know. A lot of their friends were doing more than necking. She wasn't ready. She didn't know if he would be the one she'd give herself to.

She entered the sitting room and handed Ronald his glass. She sat in the chair. They drank their colas and stared at each other. Neither could find words to say.

Ronald finished his drink and set the glass on the coaster. "I guess I better go, we've got a big day tomorrow. I'll come by in the morning to walk you to class."

"Thanks, that would be swell."

He took her hand from the doorknob placing it around his waist. He placed his hands around her face and leaned his forehead against hers. "I'll see you in the morning, beautiful."

She placed a kiss on his cheek. "See you then."

She closed the door and leaned against it. She surveyed her quarters and decided to straighten and unpack before studying. She couldn't concentrate on anything except Ronald and how he made her feel.

She imagined kissing Frankie like she did Ronald. The feel of Frankie's skin against her hand when she got in his car flitted across her mind. Her heart pounded at the memory. Why couldn't she like Ronald? She needed someone like him, not Frankie. Her mind raced as she compared the two. Frankie's tall frame and muscular physique towered over Ronald's skinny dancer's body. Ronald had a keen intelligence where Frankie was manly, tough, and street smart. She felt safer with a man like Frankie. He wouldn't back away from a fight. Not many people would mess with him. Ronald would have to talk his way out of a fight, but Frankie would jump in head first. She didn't know why she thought about Frankie. He loved Audrey and would always pine for his lost love. She was no match for Audrey's beauty. If that's the kind of girl he wanted, she didn't have a chance.

****

Ruth Ann and Ronald raced to the bulletin board for the results of the auditions. She scanned the board until she saw her name. She jumped in the air and screamed, "I got the part."

Ronald searched the list and found his name. "I did too." He kissed her.

She backed away. "Not here, Ronald."

"Sorry." He looked around. "We got our parts. You're Natalya and I'm Andrei. It's going to be fun.

We'll be together all the time."

She tugged him toward their classroom so the others could check the board. She didn't know if the empty feeling in her stomach stemmed from excitement or fear. Either way, they'd be together all the time, rehearsing. "I can't believe I got the part."

"Of course you got the part, you're the best." He let her enter the classroom ahead of him.

"I'm not surprised they chose you for Andrei, you're the best in our class. I'm surprised about getting my part. Thanks for your help, preparing me for the audition and everything." She stopped and touched his hand.

He winked. "My pleasure, beautiful."

The room buzzed with happy and disappointed students. Ruth Ann glanced around the room, if dirty looks were daggers, she'd be dead. Jenny Price hugged Ronald with a full body embrace and congratulated him. She didn't glance at Ruth Ann or acknowledge her presence. Jenny walked away with her eyes focused on Ronald. He stared and smiled. Ruth Ann was caught in a private moment between him and another girl, and she didn't like it. She punched him on the arm. "What was that about?"

Ronald rubbed his arm. "That hurt." He ignored her question as another group of girls congratulated him.

They took their seats as the teacher read the assignments. The ones who didn't get a major part were understudies, extras, or set workers. Everyone in the class had a job to do in the play. She wrote important dates on the blackboard including when lines were to be memorized, set and costume deadlines, and the date of the spring production. Ruth Ann wrote the dates in her notebook with a star beside what applied to her. The teacher congratulated everyone and reminded each student that their job, whether the star or a dresser, was important to the production of a successful play. She dismissed the class and stood at the front as students peppered her with questions.

Ruth Ann gathered her books.

Ronald glanced at Jenny before following Ruth Ann out of the classroom. "How about I buy you a burger?" He reached for her books.

She passed them to him. "Sure, thanks."

Ronald watched her devour her hamburger. "What do you want to do tonight?"

She drank a sip of cola. "I need to study. I'm going to start memorizing my lines."

"I can help you." His gaze steady and hopeful.

She didn't want another tug of war. "No, I need to be alone and study, and I promised my mother I'd write her when the results were posted."

They left the restaurant and meandered toward their living quarters. The sun dipped toward the horizon causing the temperature to drop. Ronald put his arm around her, and she plunged her hands into the pockets of her jacket. When they arrived at her door, he gathered her in his arms and kissed her good night.

She stopped him before he got carried away. "I'll see you in the morning."

He reached for her key. She placed it in his hand, he unlocked the door and waited for her to enter. "See you then."

She sat on the settee surveying the tiny apartment. She liked her living quarters. The twin bed had a better mattress than her bed at home, and the desk in the bedroom held her books and papers with space left over to write notes on her script. The kitchen had a refrigerator, stove, and small table. She had no money for luxuries like a radio, so she spent her time learning as much as she could before her year of college ended.

She tried not to think of home. She missed everyone, but Frankie more than anyone, and that surprised her. She smiled as she remembered how Ronald flinched when Frankie shook his hand. There was more to the barnstormer, and she wanted to learn all of it. She paused and whispered a prayer. She prayed he would get over his mistake of marrying Audrey and find true happiness.

Chapter Nine

Frankie turned his car into the large driveway of Andrews Field and glanced at the air sock, something he did every morning. The sock stood straight out, and dark clouds rolled in the distance. There would be no flying until the weather improved. Al stood at the tailgate of his old blue truck and waved. He parked next to Al's truck and got out of his car. "Good morning, Al."

Al grabbed a bag of rags and cleaner from his truck. "Good morning, son."

"Can I help you with anything?" He stood next to his friend and waited.

"No, I've got it, bought a few supplies in town." Al gathered his bags. "You can open the door for me."

Frankie closed the tailgate on Al's truck and opened the side door feeling the wall for the light switch. He unlocked the large hangar door but left it closed. "You making coffee this morning?"

"Heading that way now." Al put the bags in the storage room.

He sat at his desk and studied the to-do list Victor left him. He numbered each line in the order he planned to do the tasks.

Al yelled, "Coffee's ready."

He strolled to the back of the hangar where the old man had their chairs assembled. He poured a cup of coffee, sat, and sipped the hot brew. "How was your weekend? Did you see Ethel?"

"I did. She cooked dinner for me yesterday."

He watched his friend's face come to life when he mentioned Ethel. "You've been together for years. When are ya gonna marry her?"

Al sipped his coffee. He stayed quiet for several minutes. "I would marry that pretty woman in a heartbeat, but she doesn't want to. Says she likes her job at the mill, and she likes livin' with her sister. Says she's got more now than she ever had. She doesn't want nothin' to disturb her life. I can't blame her. I ain't got much to offer. She lives in a better house than I could give her."

Ruthie's face flitted through his mind. He felt the same way. She had more going for her than he ever would. "I understand. I've liked women who were too good for me, but you and Ethel love each other. I can't understand why she won't marry you."

"I believe she'd marry me if her sister got married, and they kicked her out of the house. She worries. Told me one day when I mixed moonshine with her cola." Al gave Frankie a wink. "We had a good time that day."

"I bet you did." He gave the old man a knowing smile.

Al shook his head. "Yeah, she watches me close now. What about you? Anything excitin' happen to you this weekend?"

He stood to pour more coffee in his cup. "If you call flying Her Highness Ruthie to school exciting."

"Why'd you fly her and not Victor?"

"Victor got called out on a job, so I had to. I didn't want to."

Al handed his cup to Frankie to refresh. "The feisty girl got to be alone with you, huh?"

"What do you mean?" He filled the cup and passed it to Al.

"Well, son, she searched the hangar for you while you hid in the supply room. She likes you, but she's too darn uppity to admit it. You like her and you're too gol dang stubborn. At least me and Ethel admit we love each other even though it ain't in writin'."

Frankie plucked a pack of cigarettes from his shirt pocket. He offered one to Al.

He raised his hand. "I'm trying to quit. Ethel fusses at me. She don't like the smell."

He pulled a long draw from his cigarette. "Yeah, I'd quit until this trouble with Audrey. I need one to calm me." He tapped his cigarette with his finger. The ash fell to the floor as he blew smoke into the air. "Ruthie has a boyfriend. He picked her up at the airport. He's an actor, the kind of guy she needs."

"She introduced him as her boyfriend?"

"No, but I could tell, he was all over her."

"Was she all over him?" Al drank a sip of coffee.

"No, she made sure he didn't touch her in front of me. You know how she is, a tease." He blew out smoke and rubbed the cigarette butt on the cement floor with his foot.

"She plays her cat and mouse game with you because she has eyes for you. Sounds like she doesn't like this boy. He's conveniently there, and she's lonely. Better take more time with her next time she comes home."

Frankie placed the pack of Chesterfield's on a shelf, out of sight out of mind. He hoped he could feel the same about Ruthie.

They fell into their work. Frankie on a customer's airplane while Al cleaned the bathroom.

Victor walked in the door and headed to his office. "Morning, crew. How's everyone today?"

Al waved from the bathroom where he cleaned the floor.

Frankie stepped off the small ladder. "I'm fine. How'd the flight go yesterday? Any problems with the customer?"

The boss removed his coat and hung it on his coat rack. "No problem, they enjoyed their flight. I think we'll have some repeat business. How was the flight to Atlanta?"

He trudged to Victor's office. "Fine, no problems."

"Did Ruth Ann behave? I told her not to say anything about Audrey."

"Oh, we talked about it." Frankie crossed his arms and leaned against the doorframe. "Some boy named Ronald met her."

Victor nodded, sat in his chair, and pulled the telephone directory from a drawer. "I heard about him. I can't see Ruth Ann with an actor. She needs a man who can handle her, not someone like her."

"I don't think there's a man strong enough to handle her."

Victor picked up the telephone receiver, leaned his head, and snuggled the receiver on his shoulder. "I wouldn't be too sure. I know someone who can give her a run for her money."

Victor dialed a number, his cue to get back to work. He hadn't made it a secret he wanted to date Ruthie. He didn't encourage him, but Victor knew he was stuck on his sister.

In the late afternoon, Frankie opened the hangar door to let some fresh air in. He spotted Mr. Douglas' 1932 Buick enter the lot. Lisbeth's head rose a few inches above the steering wheel.

He opened her car door and greeted her. "So, you're driving now. Mr. Douglas lets you drive his car. I'm impressed."

Lisbeth closed the car door. "He didn't want me to drive. Finally, he agreed to teach me. Said he'd rather I learned from him than a friend."

He escorted her into the hangar. "Mr. Douglas is a very smart man."

She lowered her voice, "Have you thought anymore about teaching me to fly?"

He gazed at the pretty little girl, a foot shorter than him. He couldn't imagine her flying a plane. "I wasn't sure if you were serious. Did you ask your father?"

"Not yet." Lisbeth spotted her brother in his office talking on the telephone and taking notes.

"I see. Well you better talk to Victor, 'cause I'm not getting into trouble with him or Mr. Douglas. Anyway, he has to know if I'm teaching you, he's the boss here. Go see him. I'll join you in a minute."

She hesitated then headed to her brother's office. She waited outside until he finished his telephone conversation.

Victor put his ledger aside. "Hey, Lisbeth. What brings you here?"

She sat in the chair in front of his desk. "I want to talk to you about something."

"I'm all ears." He leaned back in his chair and smiled at his sister.

She moved to the front of the chair and grinned. "I want to take flying lessons." Her voice filled with excitement.

He had to close his mouth before he could speak. "Where did you get this idea?"

"From Amelia Earhart and Louise Thaden." She picked up the latest issue of *Flying Aces* magazine. "Can I borrow this?"

"Sure." Victor watched his sister flip through the periodical. "Wait, you know who these women are?"

"Yes, I know who they are. I've read books about them and other women flyers. You aren't the only one in the family who wants to fly an airplane."

Victor noticed Frankie watching them. "Did you talk to Ma and Pa about this?"

"No, I spoke to Frankie about it at Ruth Ann's party. I want him to teach me...and you, too. Maybe I can work with you."

His gaze went from Frankie to Lisbeth. "What about college? Pa's going to be upset. You remember what a hard time he gave me, and I'm military trained." Victor stood and motioned Frankie to come in the office.

He stopped at the door. "You need me, boss?"

"Yes, come in. Seems, my little sister wants to learn to fly."

He sat and smiled at Lisbeth. "Yep, she talked to me about it at the party. If she wants to learn, I say why not?"

Victor stared at his sister. "We'll teach you but you have to get Ma and Pa's approval. Don't tell them you want to work with us instead of college. We'll take one step at a time."

She stood. "Thanks Victor. Will you talk to them?"

"How about you ask them first? If need be, I'll say something."

Lisbeth hugged her brother and Frankie before racing to the car.

Victor yelled, "Calm down. Be careful driving home."

Al stuck his head in the office. "What's goin' on?"

"My sister wants us to teach her how to fly. I told her we would if Pa and Ma approve."

Al put his hands on his hips. "What about that? Apples don't fall far from the tree now, do they?"

Chapter Ten

Ruth Ann and Ronald spent their spare time at the diner where they ran lines for the play. They sat in the back booth. The waitress didn't approach unless they waved. Ruth Ann wanted the confidence Ronald had. This was the most important thing she'd ever done in her life. Her long held dream as a stage actress, only a few short months away from becoming a reality kept her stomach in a knot. She couldn't eat, and the waist of her skirts hung at her hips. She placed her script on the Formica table. "What if we forget our lines?"

He grabbed her hand. "You won't. You practically have them memorized now."

"What if I get scared and can't remember?"

He cradled her hand in both of his. "We'll be together in most of the scenes, and I'll make sure you don't. Trust me."

She felt a tingle in the pit of her stomach. She liked Ronald, not as much as he liked her, but this did feel good. He stirred feelings, feelings she wasn't sure she could handle. "Thanks, Ronald, for everything you do for me."

He winked. "My pleasure, beautiful."

She tugged her hand from his grasp. "Guess we better get home, we have an early day tomorrow."

"I've got this." He gathered their books.

"I can carry something, you know."

He shifted the books into one hand and held Ruth Ann's hand with the other. "I know you can, but I like taking care of you."

They strolled the few blocks to the school. She unlocked her door. He followed her in, placed the books on the kitchen table, and separated his from hers.

"Can I get you anything?"

Ronald put his arm around her waist, positioning her body close to his. "Just you." His tongue separated her lips as he forged it into her mouth.

Her body was too heavy for her legs. He tightened his hold around her waist to steady her. His hands raced an urgent path along her body making her nerve endings tingle.

She would continue until the morning if all they did was neck. He wouldn't be content with kissing. She removed his hands and held them at her side while she returned his kiss with the same intensity. She relaxed her hold of his hands. He drew her close. The hardness of his arousal evident as he pressed it against her belly. She stepped back startled.

He placed her hand on his swollen shaft. "See what you do to me. God, I want you so bad."

He leaned his forehead to hers, with eyes closed he said, "Please, Ruth Ann, I love you."

She stepped back and stared into his eyes. A fever of desire swept through her, aching to be fulfilled or released, she wasn't sure which. The urgency so strong she wanted to take him to her bed. A tug of war between her brain and her emotions battled. She grasped his hand and led him to the settee. "I need to talk to you."

He sat. "You're not breaking up with me, are you?"

"No, I'm not ready for..." She paused. "I'm not ready for, Barneymugging. I'm afraid you'll break up with me if I don't."

Ronald couldn't control his burst of laughter. "Is that what you call it?"

Her face burned red. "It's what my mother calls it." She looked at him as their laughter filled the room.

Amusement flickered in his eyes as he pulled her hand into his, raised it to his lips, and kissed it. "Seriously though, I'd never force you to do anything. I can wait. I'll wait as long as I have to. I love you."

Her smile melted from her face. She didn't know what to say, did she love him? She didn't know. She would not hurt his feelings, but she didn't want to declare she loved him if she didn't. "Ronald, I love being with you, kissing you. You make me feel special."

"You're special, you're beautiful, you're talented. Everything a man could ever want. I want you to be my steady girl. Will you?"

He surprised her. She'd seen the jealous stares of the girls in their class. Ronald could have any one of them. "Yes, I'll be your steady girl if you slow down. I'm not ready..."

He smoothed her hair out of her face. "We'll go as slow as you want. I promise."

After he left, she sat on the settee, the last minutes of their tryst played through her mind. She liked Ronald and the way he made her feel was addicting. She liked the way he touched and caressed her, but she couldn't give her body...yet. She had to be careful, she wasn't in Saplingville and he wasn't one of her small town boyfriends. She liked the idea of going steady with him, it eased her loneliness. He might be the one. She tore a piece of paper from her tablet. She wrote her ma a letter to tell her family about Ronald.

Chapter Eleven

Jacob Douglas stepped out of his car and waved to Frankie. "Afternoon, I need to talk to you and Victor."

Frankie knew they were either going to be chewed out for talking to Lisbeth about flying or lectured on the safety of teaching a teenager how to fly. Mr. Douglas didn't mince words. "Afternoon, Mr. Douglas, how are you?"

"I was fine until my youngest daughter informed me she wanted to fly an airplane."

He put his screw driver on the bench and wiped his hands, the grease smeared into his skin. "Yes, she surprised us too. Let me wash up. I'll meet you in Victor's office."

Frankie scrubbed his hands and listened, no yelling was a good sign. He felt like a kid called to the principal's office. He wished Victor would handle this and tell him about it later. Mr. Douglas had his hands full. His daughters were the two most independent, headstrong girls he'd ever met. Ruthie got her way about acting school, so he figured Lisbeth would win her fight, too. He took his time to give his boss a moment alone with his father.

He watched Al fill the percolator with water. "Thanks. We'll need the pot along with three cups."

"Will do." The old man nodded and went about his business.

He entered the office as Mr. Douglas asked, "How did this start? Did either of you say anything to Lisbeth to get this idea in her head?"

Victor nodded at Frankie. "I didn't know anything until she rode by here a few days ago to ask if we would teach her. Said she'd talked to Frankie about lessons at Ruth Ann's party."

Frankie chose his words before responding. *They can't blame me for this.* "Lisbeth asked if I would teach her how to fly, and I told her she would have to get permission from you and Mrs. Douglas. I was as surprised as you both are."

Victor regarded his father. "We talked. She seems to have done a lot of research on women aviators. I believe she has considered this a long time. I say we give her a few lessons. She'll get it out of her system, or she'll be too afraid to solo."

Mr. Douglas crossed his arms across his chest. "Yes, I hoped you'd get it out of your system flying in the service, made you want to fly more."

Al entered the office with coffee. Frankie grabbed the pot and poured the hot brew into cups. He wanted the boss to do the talking. He would respond if he had to. He respected Mr. Douglas, but Victor was as stubborn as his father, he'd let them duke it out.

Victor cradled his cup in both hands. "What did Lisbeth tell you?"

"Lisbeth announced she wanted to learn to fly, said she had talked to you and Frankie, and you agreed to teach her."

Victor dropped his cup from his mouth spilling coffee on his shirt. He opened his drawer and grabbed a handkerchief. "Partly true. She talked to us. We agreed to teach her if you and Ma approve."

"Well, I'm glad you cleared that up." Jacob blew on the coffee before taking a sip. "I think she has a good head on her shoulders. She's smart and more mature than Ruth Ann is, even with the age difference."

Victor agreed, "Lisbeth's smart. I think she's mature enough to fly. We'll make sure she does everything by the book."

Frankie sipped his coffee and thought about Ruthie. She was a trouble maker and immature. He hoped she would be all right in Atlanta. He'd like to put Ronald in his place. *If he hurts Ruthie...* Victor called his name. He gave his boss his attention. "Yes."

Victor stared, giving him a questioning look. "What do you think?"

He put his cup on the desk. "Lisbeth's very intelligent. I know she'd be a good student. Remember at her age, I flew with the barnstormers. You started lessons before you joined the service. I think she's old enough."

Mr. Douglas regarded them with a stern gaze. "I will agree to a few lessons. Let's see if she likes it. I'm hoping she won't. You tell me how she does. If she makes mistakes or doesn't comprehend, stop the lessons. She'll be in college soon, and she'll forget about this nonsense."

Victor and Frankie both said, "Agreed" at the same time. Their eyes met, he understood his boss's signal and stood. The conversation was over.

Mr. Douglas left the hangar, and Al joined them with an empty cup. Frankie filled the cup with coffee. The old man sat, and they hashed over the conversation.

Al studied the coffee in his cup. "Well, did the

little girl get her way?"

Victor nodded. "Yes, I haven't seen much she asked my father for she didn't get."

Frankie set his cup on the desk. "Please don't tell him she wants to work with us instead of going to college."

"Don't worry," Victor replied. "Let's keep that bit of information between the three of us."

Al set his cup on the desk and leaned forward. "Reckon when she's gonna want to start her lessons?"

Victor leaned in his chair and put his hands behind his head. "If I know Lisbeth, tomorrow won't be soon enough. Frankie, get ready, she wants to learn from you first."

"Yes, she told me. Whatcha want to start her in?"

Victor thought for a moment. "I'd like to start her in the Jenny. It'd be her first and last lesson. Let's give her a chance. We'll start her in the Cessna. I want detailed notes on her flight time and what she learns in each lesson. If she does decide to solo, we'll have all the information we need to get her certified. We'll treat her like any client. I think Pa's wrong, she won't quit. When she decides she wants something, she follows through, like he does."

Frankie observed Victor as he talked about the lessons, energy filled the room. "You sound excited."

"You betcha. We're making history here. How many women pilots do you know? I've read about them, but I don't know any. I'm proud of her."

Frankie agreed, "I don't know any either. Lisbeth can do whatever she sets her mind to. I'll help any way I can."

Frankie and Al left the office and headed to work.

Al grabbed his broom and started sweeping. "Went better than I thought."

Frankie stuck his head in the airplane engine. "Yeah, it did."

He concentrated on the engine repair. He could block Ruthie out of his mind most of the time, but when he was with any of her family, she flooded his thoughts. He needed a distraction. He was leery about going to the next town to meet women. That's where he ran into Audrey. He had depleted his supply of women in Saplingville. Most of the girls he dated were married now. Ruthie didn't care about him; she had her pick of boys. Ronald wasn't the only classmate sniffing around her. He was sure.

Chapter Twelve

Lisbeth arrived at the hangar for her lesson. Frankie had the yellow Cessna fueled and ready to go. "For your first lesson, we're going to get familiar with the airplane. Let's walk around the plane. There's some things you need to know."

Lisbeth ran her hand along the side of the airplane. "Thanks for doing this. I'm so excited Pa allowed you and Victor to teach me."

He reviewed the safety check list and passed it to Lisbeth. "You're welcome. I can tell this means a lot to you, and I'm happy to be your instructor." He led her toward the tail end of the airplane. "First, safety's the most important thing about flying. You have to know your airplane is in good shape before you take off. We always go through a check list so we don't forget anything. Study the list and check off anything listed when we get to it." He gave her a pencil. "You'll learn in this airplane first because it's the most stable one we have. As you see, the wings are mounted high. They are made of all wood. The fuselage is steel tubing with wooden stringers and formers and the tail surfaces are wooden covered with plywood."

Lisbeth interrupted him, "Do I need to know how the plane is constructed, isn't this information more for a mechanic or builder?"

He shook his head. "No, you need to know

everything you can about the planes you fly because if something happens in the air, you know the plane inside and out. If you have to make an emergency landing, for instance, the Jenny would respond differently from this plane."

"Okay, I see your point. I'd love to fly the Jenny someday, too."

"Oh, you will. I wouldn't miss teaching you to fly the JN-Four."

They strolled around the airplane several times with Frankie explaining the purpose of each control surface: wings, ailerons, elevators, rudder, and propeller. They checked the tires, oil, and gasoline. She checked off everything on the list. They climbed into the airplane, Lisbeth in the pilot seat.

Frankie said, "I want you to watch me today. When we achieve our altitude, I'll let you fly a little."

She watched him. "What's the altitude in this plane?"

"We'll fly at about five thousand feet today."

Frankie taxied to the runway. He helped her complete the before take-off check list. Lining up on the runway center line, he added full power and made a smooth takeoff. He watched his student. She held her hand out and mimicked his movements. He raised his voice above the engine noise. "Place your hand on your control stick. Feel how the plane responds when I maneuver the stick." The plane dipped and rose at his command. "Feel how steady the airplane is now? I'm holding the stick steady. You give it a try."

He removed his hands from the stick. The plane started dipping. He advised her. "Make small corrections, *small* corrections, got it?"

She didn't panic. "Yes, got it." She steadied the control stick.

"That's it. You've got a knack for this. I'll let you fly the plane for a while." He watched the spunky girl as she followed his instructions. "Time to turn back, I'll take the controls now, and you watch as we head to the airfield for our descent."

"Victor says you make the smoothest landings." She watched the gauges.

"He's not so bad himself. I had to land with wing walkers on the wings. I didn't want to get anyone killed."

"I remember going with Victor and Uncle Walter to see a flying circus when I was a little girl. Uncle Walter paid extra for Victor to fly in one of the airplanes. I wanted to go, but they had an age limit." She watched Frankie maneuver the airplane into a smooth landing on the airstrip.

"Well, you aren't too young now. You're the best student I've ever had. You'll be taking off and landing soon enough." He taxied toward the hangar.

Victor sauntered to the airplane opening the door for his sister. "How was your first lesson?"

"Wonderful, when can I take another one?" She jumped out and hugged her brother.

He raised his eyebrows, and Frankie gave a nod. "How about one lesson a week?"

She hugged Frankie. "Thank you, I'll see you next week."

Frankie and Victor headed into the hangar while Lisbeth backed Jacob's car from the parking space. "She did great boss. She's a natural, like her brother."

Victor ran his hand through his hair. "I'm not

surprised, but I think Pa will be. We'll cross that bridge when we get there."

Chapter Thirteen

Ruth Ann and Ronald were asked to perform part of their lines for their Method's Class. The teacher demonstrated how Constantin Stanislavski approached acting. Today they were working on emotion memory. They were instructed to remember something in their past and bring that emotion to the surface during their performance. Ronald played the part of Ruth Ann's love interest Andrei. She concentrated on the technique, and her thoughts drifted to Frankie. She shoved his memory from her mind.

The teacher screamed, "What is wrong with you? You are terrible. Grasp the emotion of the part."

Her face flushed. She shook with anger.

The teacher said in a calm voice, "Yes, yes I see your emotion. Good. Now, think of the man you love, embrace him in your heart. Let us see your emotion."

She closed her eyes and let her thoughts drift. She pictured the barnstormer in his leather coat and goggles taking off in the Jenny. The airplane soared above her, and she twirled around, around, around, staring at the biplane sail through the sky. She recited her lines to Ronald. The teacher nodded in approval, the classroom erupted in applause.

Ronald hugged her and whispered, "This part was made for us. The fact we love each other, helps, too."

She was an impostor, lying and cheating her way

through the play. She didn't care; if it worked, she'd do it. "Yes, it helps."

"What were you thinking about?" They strolled to their seat in the middle of the theater.

Frankie. "You tell me first."

"I thought about last night and your tantalizing kisses. Now you." Ronald whispered in her ear.

"I used the same memory," she lied.

The class ended. She grabbed her books and exited the theater with Ronald. "I wrote my mother a letter to tell her about you. I hoped we could go to Saplingville Sunday so I could introduce you to them."

He stared at her with a surprised smile on his face, "I would love to meet your family. How long is the drive?"

"A little over two hours. Do you think it's too far to go in one day?"

"Not at all."

"I'll call Ma to tell her we're coming."

Ruth Ann doubted herself after she'd asked Ronald. She feared she used him to take her home because she wanted to see her family. Her mother would like him, and that knowledge didn't sit well in the pit of her stomach.

****

Sunday morning, she dressed and sat at her desk studying. A knock on the door interrupted her thoughts. She peeked out the window, Ronald stood on the door step wearing a suit and tie. She grabbed her purse before opening the door. "Good morning, Ronald, you look dapper."

"What a pretty dress." He stepped inside.

"This is one of my Sunday dresses. I've never seen

you in a suit either."

"Had to dress my best for your family. Ready to go?"

She followed him to his car and ran her hand over the fender of the fancy automobile.

Ronald opened the door. She settled into his light blue Studebaker. "I appreciate you taking me to see my parents."

"I know you miss them. I miss mine, too. Can't wait to have Sunday dinner with your family."

She watched him maneuver the car onto the two lane road toward Saplingville. "I want you to see my little town. I hope you like it."

"I'm sure I will, I don't think it'll be different from Montgomery, Alabama, a little smaller, I suppose."

She enjoyed the long ride and talking to Ronald away from the prying eyes of her classmates. They had a lot in common. Before she knew it, they arrived at the Saplingville, Georgia sign.

He slowed the car. "We're here."

She scooted to the edge of her seat. "Turn here, let's ride down Main Street, I want you to see the Drug Store."

He made a right turn. "There it is. Douglas Drug Store…nice. When did your father open it?"

"Nineteen oh five. Look, across the street is Murphy's Five and Dime. Dottie, Victor's wife, worked there when they met. Turn right at the next street. We live on the second street to the left, two eighty-three Vine Street."

He eased the car into the driveway.

Hattie raced out the front door, grabbed her in a quick hug. She held her daughter at arm's length. "I've been watching for you."

Ronald stood at the front of the car.

She took her mother's hand. "Ma, I want you to meet Ronald Waters."

Hattie shook his hand. "Pleased to meet you, Ronald. Welcome to our home."

Jacob and Lisbeth waited in the house. She grabbed her boyfriend's arm dragging him in the parlor. "Pa, Lisbeth, I want you to meet Ronald Waters."

Mr. Douglas rose from his chair and shook his hand. "Pleased to make your acquaintance."

Lisbeth stood. "I've heard a lot about you, nice to meet you."

Ronald acknowledged both. "The pleasure's all mine. I've heard lots about all of you."

Jacob motioned toward a chair. "Please, sit. Tell us about yourself."

Ronald sat in the chair opposite Mr. Douglas and the girls sat on the sofa.

"Not much to tell. I'm from Montgomery, Alabama. Ruth Ann and I met at school. I've wanted to be an actor since I was a young boy."

"What does your father do for a living?"

"He's a lawyer, and my mother teaches school."

Jacob studied the young man. "How did they feel about you wanting to become an actor?"

"They support my decision. I've taken dancing and singing lessons since seven years old, and I play the guitar. I don't think they were surprised at my choice of profession."

Ruth Ann interrupted, "Ronald's the best in our class. We both got lead parts in the spring production. I hope you can come and see us perform."

Hattie waltzed into the parlor. "Of course, we will."

She lowered her voice and addressed her mother. "Who's coming for dinner today?"

Lisbeth spoke, "Victor, Dottie, and the kids. Anyone else you want to invite?"

She closed her eyes and thanked God they didn't invite Frankie. "No. I've missed those babies, can't wait to see them."

Lisbeth stood. "It's not too late to invite one of your friends. I saw Frankie last week. He gave me my first flying lesson."

She reined in her temper, given enough rope her sister would spoil her day with Ronald. "How was your first lesson?"

"Fantastic. Frankie's a great teacher."

Ronald cradled Ruth Ann's hand in his. "Yes, Frankie flew you to Atlanta. Nice fellow."

She had to end the conversation. "Yes, he works for Victor. Ma, do you need help with anything?"

"I've got to stir my beans before they burn and stick to the pan." Hattie raced toward the kitchen.

Ruth Ann followed her mother. She heard Victor's car doors slam. She ran out the back door to meet them.

She hugged her brother and Dottie. Carol Ann and Jack Andrew put their little arms out. "Who shall I take first?" She pulled Carol Ann into her arms. She kissed the baby boy's hand and tickled his belly. "I've missed you two so much." She escorted Victor's family to the parlor to meet her new boyfriend. "Ronald, this is my brother Victor, his wife Dottie, and their twins."

Victor shook Ronald's hand. "Nice to meet you. I'm glad Ruth Ann found a friend in Atlanta. We worry about her alone in the big city."

Victor sat on the sofa with Ronald. The girls helped Hattie in the kitchen.

Jacob nodded to Victor. "Ronald and I were talking about his family. His father's a lawyer in Montgomery, Alabama."

Victor addressed the man. "Any siblings?"

"No. My parents were too busy for more, I guess. My mother's a teacher."

Victor asked, "What are your plans after you graduate?"

"Headed to New York. I've always wanted to be a stage actor. They say it's the place to go."

Jacob grunted. "I hope you don't give my daughter any ideas. I agreed for her to go to acting school. I did not agree to her moving to New York."

Victor changed the subject. "I hear my sis got a good part in the upcoming production."

Ronald grinned. "Yes, we both got lead parts. We play love interests in Anton Chekhov's play, *The Three Sisters*."

Jacob started coughing. Victor raced to the kitchen to get him some water.

Ruth Ann asked her brother, "How's it going?"

"Not good. I think you need to join us to keep peace between Pa and Ronald."

"Oh, dear." She passed Carol Ann to Lisbeth.

They hurried to the parlor as Hattie reminded, "Dinner'll be ready in ten minutes."

Ruth Ann entered the room as Ronald said, "I'm in love with your daughter, Mr. Douglas." She put her hand on her heart. *Oh, dear Lord I can't leave them alone together.*

Her father glared. "You met her for the first time in September, for goodness sake."

She stared at Victor; he enjoyed this. Remorse for the trouble she'd given her brother swept over her. She wanted him to say something, anything. When he didn't, she regained control of the situation. "Ma says dinner's ready in ten minutes. We're having meat loaf, it's one of your favorites, Pa."

Jacob stood and scowled at his daughter. "I'll wash my hands."

Victor kept the conversation going. "So, you're in love with Ruth Ann, huh?"

Ronald nodded his head and smiled. "She's the best."

She wanted to take her hand from his grasp, retreat to her bedroom, and hide.

Victor gave her a wink. "Are you in love, little sister?"

She gave him a look to stop a clock but when Ronald faced her, she smiled. "I told Ronald, I like him and I love being with him. We're taking it slow, aren't we?"

Ronald placed her hair behind her ear. "Whatever you say, beautiful."

On the ride to Atlanta, Ronald was gay. He overflowed with excitement about meeting her family. "This has been a swell day. Your family's the best, thanks for suggesting this."

I missed my family and wanted to see them. What a mistake taking him with me. "Yeah, thanks for driving me home today."

Everyone treated Ronald with respect, but he didn't fit in like she'd hoped. Hattie kissed her on the cheek when they left and whispered, "Now, Ruth Ann, be a good girl, you hear me?" Boy, if she knew how hard that was. Victor talked to Ronald and included him in their conversations, but she could tell he wasn't impressed. She could have kicked Lisbeth, talking about Frankie in front of him. All's well that ends well. At least Ronald didn't have a clue.

He parked his car on the street in front of her building. He grabbed her hand. "Can I come in?"

She kissed his cheek. "No, I'm tired. I had a great time. Thank you for taking me home."

He brushed her lips with a kiss. "My pleasure. I enjoyed meeting your family, they're nice."

She couldn't meet his eye, so she whispered in his ear. "They liked you, too."

"I hope so. Your father gave me the third degree about us."

"Yes, I heard. He worries about me."

"I let him know that I'd take care of you."

That was your mistake. She smiled and kissed his cheek. "I'll see you tomorrow."

"See you then, beautiful."

She closed the door and stood with her forehead against it.

What was I thinking? She gave her mother ammunition. Hattie wouldn't rest until she married Ronald. At least she didn't live at home and have to listen to her every day.

Chapter Fourteen

Frankie sat in his chair reading the Sunday paper. A reflection on the wall caught his eye. He peered from the window as Victor and his family wandered to his front porch. He opened the door and greeted them. "What do I owe this pleasure?"

Victor handed Jack Andrew to Frankie. "We were in the neighborhood and thought you'd like to see the babies."

He settled Carol Ann on his other hip and hugged both. "Boy, they're getting big. I can't wait until they start walking."

Dottie tugged the babies' sweaters off. "I can wait. They're going to run me to death. I have to corral them in the parlor now. They crawl all over the house if I don't."

Frankie sat on the sofa bouncing a baby on each knee. "What have y'all been doin'?"

Victor watched his babies laugh and try to crawl over Frankie. "We had lunch with my parents. Ruth Ann blew into town for the day."

He put the babies on the floor. He got on his hands and knees crawling around with them. "How'd she get here?"

Victor sat on the couch next to Dottie and held her hand. "Ronald drove her."

Frankie gathered the twins close to his side. "Are

they serious?"

"You know my sister. Ronald's serious about her, Ruth Ann not so much."

"Did y'all like him?"

Victor gazed at his wife.

She gave him a stern glare. "He seems like a nice boy."

Victor corrected, "You mean a nice man. I don't think he has a chance with my sister. He's too nice. She'll run all over him. You know how headstrong she is."

He stepped into his bedroom and grabbed the sock monkeys he kept for the kids. "It could work. They have a lot in common. They both want to be actors."

Victor shook his head. "There is such a thing as being too much alike. My bull-headed sister needs someone with balls."

Dottie put her hand over his mouth. "Victor, please watch what you say in front of the babies."

"They're babies, Dottie."

"Yes, babies now, but they listen to every word. I don't want them repeating some of the things you say. You need to start practicing reducing your vocabulary...now."

"Yes, ma'am."

He loved how Dottie could reel Victor in with a word. His friend loved his wife and kids. Frankie admired them. He'd hoped for the same life with Audrey. He had to accept the fact he would never have what Victor did. "Who knows. Maybe she'll marry him, and they'll move to New York."

"Ronald told my father he wanted to take her to New York. You should have seen Pa's face."

"What'd Mr. Douglas say?"

"Pa said he agreed to let Ruth Ann go to acting school, but he sure didn't agree to her moving to New York and for him not to give her any ideas."

Frankie felt a kinship with Mr. Douglas. "So he didn't like him?"

"No, I don't think my father took to Ronald Waters. The thing he liked about him is his father's a lawyer. You know how Pa is with intellectuals."

His father's a lawyer. He has so much more to offer her than I do. "Well, I guess Ruthie has the last word, doesn't she?"

Dottie spoke, "She does, it's not the business of her brother and his best friend who she marries."

Victor smiled at his wife and rubbed her cheek with his hand. "I agree. But you have no idea of the hard time she gave us."

"Yes, she's quite the actress." Frankie remembered the mixed signals she gave him. Come hither looks one minute and smart aleck remarks the next.

He sat on the floor with his legs stretched in front. The twins crawled along his legs to his face both trying to get his full attention. They stood, one on each side. He steadied them with his arms. They both grabbed a hand full of his hair and yanked. "Yikes, I guess you both like to pull hair."

Dottie ran to Frankie, grabbed their hands, and released them from his hair. "They fight over their red blocks. They've discovered the bright color."

He handed the stuffed toys to the kids. He left Dottie to deal with them. "Can I get you something to drink?"

Victor shook his head. "No, I don't want anything,

I'm full from lunch."

Dottie placed the sock monkeys on the coffee table. "We need to head home. They haven't had a nap today. They're getting cranky. Great to see you, Frankie."

"Good to see you, too. I see this goon every day." He enveloped her in a bear hug.

"Watch it buster. You're talking about your boss." He helped his wife wrestled the kids into their sweaters.

"Sorry, boss. Thanks for dropping by to see me."

Victor loaded his family into his car. He watched the Ford turn on the next street and returned to his front room through the screen door. The only sound in the house was the tick of the mantel clock sitting on a shelf. He turned on the radio to silence the quiet.

****

Al had the coffee and the chairs ready when Frankie arrived at work. He handed Frankie a cup. "How was your weekend?"

He drank a sip, *strong and hot*. "Uneventful until Victor and Dottie stopped by yesterday afternoon. How was yours?"

"Swell. Saturday night, I took Ethel to the picture show and to supper at the A&W. Did you do anything?"

"No, almost drove to the tavern, wasn't in the mood." He stretched his long legs.

Al studied him. "You need to get out, meet some new women."

"Yeah, guess I'm not ready yet. Victor said Ruthie blew into town yesterday with that Ronald fellow."

Al raised an eyebrow. "Oh?"

"Victor says he's from a prominent family from Alabama."

Al sat in his chair. "Where in Alabama?"

"Montgomery, his father's a lawyer. Looks like he comes from money. He has a lot to offer." Frankie gulped the last sip of coffee in his cup.

"You know all that glitters ain't gold. He might have a lot to offer, but if Ruth Ann doesn't want it." Al held out his cup.

He poured himself a refill and filled Al's to the rim. "I wonder if Ruthie'll ever know what she wants."

"She's a flighty little thing, that's for sure. This Ronald feller may have some money. You and I know money don't buy love or happiness. She's going to be a tough woman to please. She needs a strong man with balls."

Frankie swallowed a mouthful of coffee. Some of it felt like it went down his windpipe. He cleared his throat and coughed. "Victor's exact words."

"Well, Mr. Balls, appears you're gonna have your hands full."

"She doesn't care about me."

Al stood gathering the cups and pot. "Son, you are in denial."

He sat in his chair reflecting on their conversation. Did Al want to make him feel good about himself so he would go out and meet women, or did he see something he didn't? He'd give anything to have Ruthie in his arms and kiss her lips until she melted like candle wax. He wanted to know how making love to someone you loved and cherished made you feel. He was a red blooded man. He loved sex. Sex with love, now, that must be the grandest feeling in the world. Audrey was the sexiest woman he'd ever met. He'd gone from sex every night to never. He would wait for love this time around.

****

Frankie watched out the door for Lisbeth. He had her flight log and the pre-flight check list ready. Today the lesson plan included take offs. It was a crisp fall day, the sky powder blue with a few white clouds. Perfect day to fly.

She parked her father's Buick next to Al's truck. Frankie opened her car door. "Ready for your lesson?"

Lisbeth skipped toward the Cessna. "Can't wait. Flying's all I've thought about."

When the preliminaries were done, they sat in the plane. "Lisbeth, put your hand on the stick and feel the motion when we take off."

She followed Frankie's orders. The plane lifted from the runway. "Easy enough."

He turned and gave her a big smile. "Easy because I had the controls. We're going to fly around, return, land, and take off several times."

He watched Lisbeth concentrate, she relaxed into the movement of the stick and executed a smooth take off. "Great, I think you've got it. Next time, you take the controls."

Frankie landed the plane. Victor stood outside the hangar watching them. He pointed to Lisbeth and Victor gave a thumb's up. "Okay, Lisbeth, your turn. Remember, small corrections." He held on to the stick until she gained control. "Excellent, take the plane to five thousand, watch your compass, and head west."

Lisbeth kept her hand on the stick glancing at the controls. She spoke above the engine noise. "Ruth Ann showed up Sunday with Ronald."

Frankie's grip on the stick tightened. "I heard."

"I guess Victor told you, huh?"

"Yep." He relaxed his hold and let her take full control.

"I wish you could have heard Pa giving Ronald the third degree. My sister squirmed like a worm on a hook." She glanced at the gauges.

"He may be the one, they have a lot in common." He stared straight ahead.

"Ronald isn't her type." She turned to face him.

"What is her type?" He glanced at Lisbeth.

"You."

He shook his head and wrote in the log book. "I'm not her type she doesn't give me a second thought."

Lisbeth kept the stick steady and checked the instrument panel. "Oh, yes she does. Why do you think she argues with you?"

"Because she doesn't like me?" He watched Lisbeth handle the airplane. *She is good.*

"No, bickering is her way of getting your attention without admitting she likes you. I think she was disappointed you weren't at Sunday dinner." She smiled at him.

"Yeah, sorry I missed it." He completed his notes and put the log book behind his seat.

"She kept asking me if anyone else would be there."

I'm glad I didn't see them together. I don't like Ronald any better than Mr. Douglas does. "I'm sure she didn't miss me, she had her family and Ronald. What more could she want? Let's turn around, the hour's over. I've got some work to do before I go home. Turn the plane around and head east." He watched Lisbeth command the Cessna.

She concentrated on the stick and the compass. "Are all planes this easy to fly?"

Frankie shook his head and smiled. "No, wait until you fly the JN-Four."

"I can't wait. What's the difference?"

"Difficult to see out, especially when you're taxiing. You taxi to the runway in a zig zag pattern so you can see if anything's in your way. On the take off you glance from side to side until you get the tail up so you can see."

"What will we do in the next lesson?"

He related to her excitement remembering his first lessons in the JN-Four. "We'll practice take offs. Unlike today, you'll have total control."

Frankie landed the plane. Victor strolled toward the Cessna and waited for them to get out. "How was the lesson?"

Lisbeth hugged her brother. "Great. Did you see me take off?"

Victor kissed her head, "I did, great job."

"I got to fly the plane and turn around and head home."

He handed Victor the flight log. "She's a natural, like her brother."

"See you next week." Lisbeth ran to her car.

They entered the hangar. Frankie assembled his tools to work on an engine. "She's doing great, Victor. I've never had a student who learned as much in a short time."

"If I know Lisbeth, she's reading books about flying. She'll be teaching us a thing or two." Victor placed the flight log on a shelf and walked to his office.

Frankie started his work, it helped quiet his mind.

Anytime anyone mentioned Ruthie, hours would pass before he could stop thinking about her. He didn't think she could be any prettier. However, as she got older, she became more beautiful. Whoever married her would be a lucky man.

Chapter Fifteen

Ronald dipped a biscuit in his beef stew. "This is delicious. Thanks for cooking supper."

"Figured we'd have more time to rehearse if we ate here. Time's going by fast. We'll be headed home next week for Christmas." Ruth Ann drank a sip of tea.

"Well, you're beautiful, and you can cook. What more could a man ask for." He reached for the large bowl and spooned a second helping.

"My mother taught me. She always wanted me to settle down and get married and be like her."

He reached for her hand. "Nothing wrong with that."

She tugged her hand away, "Yes. There is. I don't want to settle down. I want to work as an actress or an acting teacher. I don't know... I want to be more than a wife."

"Why not both? You don't have to choose one or the other."

"You do if you have children." She placed the spoon in her empty bowl.

"Not necessarily. You can get people to help you with your kids. Baby, if this works between us, we can live in New York and be stage actors."

She searched Ronald's face, she envied him. He knew what he wanted. "I've dreamed of living in New York since I started reading Theatre Arts Magazines.

Now, all I want to do is go home."

"I think you're homesick. We could give New York a try. If it doesn't work, we'll move to Saplingville."

She forced a smile. *We? Will Ronald make me happy?* "Let's get busy working, we can talk about this later."

She placed the left over stew in the refrigerator. He pulled her into an embrace and kissed her. "Ronald, stop. We have to work on our lines."

He led her to the settee. She grabbed her script. "I'll sit in the chair, you sit there. It'll work better this way."

"Whatever you say, beautiful."

They plowed through the play. She missed a few lines. "I've almost got this memorized. I'll take it with me so I can learn the rest at home."

Ronald stood. He swept her close and kissed the top of her head. "I'll miss you. We should be together at Christmas."

She didn't want him in Saplingville; she wanted to be alone with her family. "Your family would miss you if you spent Christmas with me, and my mother would kill me if I wasn't home."

He kissed her and tilted her head so he could see her face. "I love you."

She gazed into his eyes and smiled. "Thanks for all the stuff you do for me. You make everything fun."

"Right back atcha. See you tomorrow."

She cleaned the kitchen scrubbing the counter until it gleamed. No matter how many times Ronald said he loved her, she didn't believe him, the words came too easy. They'd known each other three months, and he was an actor. She would wait, see how things were after the Christmas break. He must have a girlfriend in Montgomery. Two weeks will give him time to rekindle the relationship. A plan formulated in her brain she wanted to pursue when she got home. It involved a handsome barnstormer.

Chapter Sixteen

Ruth Ann stood in the crowded terminal watching for one of Victor's planes. She saw the red airplane land, and Frankie got out. She grabbed her suitcases and raced to meet him. She had an urge to hug him. She dropped her suitcases to the ground.

Without making eye contact, Frankie lumbered toward her and gathered her cases. "How did you get here, did you take a taxi?"

She wanted to lie. "No, Ronald dropped me off on his way home to Alabama."

"I see." He walked beside her keeping his gaze anywhere but on her.

She wanted to make Frankie as jealous of Ronald as she was of Audrey. "Yes, we longed to spend Christmas together, but you know how families are."

He threw her suitcases in the back of the plane. "No, I don't know how families are, I don't have one."

She hated to hit below the belt; he didn't deserve it. "You have a family, Victor and you are like brothers, and Ma thinks of you as a son."

He extended his hand and helped her into her seat. "Yes, you're right. I'm lucky to have Victor and his family."

Frankie readied for take-off. The Beechcraft Staggerwing ascended into the air in the direction of Saplingville. He raised his voice above the engine noise. "How's school? I hear you're in a play this spring."

"Yes, the end of March. I have a lead role."

"I heard Ronald's your love interest in the play, that's convenient."

She recognized contempt in his tone. "Yes, it is, makes acting the part easier."

"Doesn't that take some of the fun out of acting?"

It's acting because in real life I have to fight him off. But in the play, I pretend I want him to love me. "No, acting's always fun for me." Now was her time, butterflies fluttered in her stomach, but she had to get the dig in. "What about you, heard from Audrey?"

He inhaled a deep breath and blew it out. "No, and I don't expect to ever hear from her again."

A feeling of jealousy started at her feet and rose through her body. "I'm sure you miss her." She glanced hoping for a reaction to confirm her suspicion. "Talk about an actress, she played the part of a sexy gold digger perfectly."

"Good Lord, Ruthie, you really know how to beat a dead horse to death." He glared and narrowed his eyes. "I don't want to discuss this with you. It's a part of my life I want to forget. We've talked about this already, you said you wouldn't bring it up again."

She saw the hurt in his face. "I won't say anything more."

"Fine." Frankie concentrated on flying the airplane.

She leaned her head on the seat and closed her eyes. The tension in the cockpit thick as her mother's potato soup. She peeked at Frankie's tall frame filling the pilot seat. He commanded the airplane with confidence and skill. She stared at his handsome profile and imagined kissing him. A longing swept through her, and she fidgeted in her seat. Frankie'd been her secret fantasy since her sixteenth birthday party. A summer night she'd never forget. They were at Uncle Walter's for a hayride. The mule got spooked. and the wagon jerked, she'd almost ended up in his lap. Their eyes locked, longing swept through her body. Since that day, every time she was with Frankie, thought about Frankie, or someone mentioned Frankie, a cloud of longing and desire seeped into her core.

He worked as a mill hand at the Spangler Cotton Mill. She pegged him for an ignorant mill worker, but as she got older, she saw him for what he was. Frankie Howard, a handsome, strong-willed, smart man who could do anything he set his mind to. He didn't finish high school because he ran away with the flying circus, but he was well read and knew more about current events than she did.

Ruth Ann drifted to sleep and woke when Frankie silenced the engine of the airplane. "We got here quick. I'm glad I missed the landing. It scares me to land and take-off."

"I didn't know. I thought you liked to fly." He unfastened his seat belt.

"I do, after we're in the air and before we land." She waited for him to come around and help her out of the plane.

His Ford coupe sat alone in the parking lot. He put her suitcases in the car and headed into the hangar. "I have a couple of things to do before I take you home, I won't be long."

She followed him. She roamed the building to make sure Al wasn't hiding. "I'll wait in here with you." Her heart raced with excitement while her stomach quivered from nerves. She wanted to kiss him, wanted him to kiss her.

Frankie stepped to his desk and studied a piece of paper.

She followed him, took the paper out of his hand, and placed it on the desk. She captured his hands and placed them around her waist.

He stepped back. "What're ya doin'?"

She tiptoed and put her hands behind his neck and pulled his head toward her. She kissed him. The touch of his lips sent a shock wave through her body. He took control and devoured her mouth in a demanding kiss. She reveled in his scent. He smelled like musk, spice, motor oil, and the sky. The stubble of his beard felt rough on her lips, his strong arms enveloped her, crushing her to him. His nearness and the feel of his erection against her belly gave her nerve and confidence to do what she did next. She placed her hand on his swollen shaft and tugged upward until she was at the top, then she squeezed. Her pulse raced, her entire body filled with a want of something new and foreign to her.

Frankie scowled and stared into her eyes. "You play with fire and you're gonna get burned. You wanna do this?"

She stepped aside and met his glare with one of her own. She stared into his eyes, their souls mingled in a dance.

Frankie let out the breath he'd been holding. "No, I didn't think so. I'm taking you home."

The room spun around her, and her legs gave way. His strong arms lifted her.

His eyes filled with water and his hands trembled. "Let's go."

He kept his arm around her as they approached his car. He opened the door, helped her in the seat, bent at the waist, and gave her a gentle kiss on her mouth. "You don't know how long I've wanted to kiss you."

She searched his eyes, lost in the moment. "Probably as long as I've wanted to kiss you." She settled in her seat. She didn't open her eyes until the car stopped in her driveway. He escorted her to the front porch, depositing her suitcases by the door and left.

****

Ruth Ann couldn't sleep. She relived Frankie's kiss, the feel of his hard body against hers and the recognition that in his arms was where she wanted to remain, always. She couldn't believe her nerve. She'd never felt faint when Ronald kissed her, but she couldn't even stand without Frankie's help. What did he think of her now? She felt embarrassed, but she wasn't sorry. If she did marry Ronald, at least she knew what kissing Frankie felt like. It was all she ever dreamed of and more. What would making love with him be like? If she settled for Ronald, she would always wonder.

Chapter Seventeen

Frankie kept his confusion at bay until he delivered Ruthie home. He deposited her at her door and drove to Joe's Tavern, he needed something to calm his nerves and relax him. She had him wound as tight as a tick on a dog's back. God, he wanted her. He'd loved her for so long. What kind of sick game did she play now? If he was another man who didn't love her like he did, he would have taken advantage of her on his desk. Maybe she was already spooning with Ronald and wanted to compare the two of them. Ronald makin' whoopee with Ruthie made his stomach lurch. *The bastard better keep his hands off her.*

He had to get control. They had advanced to grown-up games. More was at stake now, like his livelihood. He wouldn't do anything to jeopardize Victor's trust.

****

Sunday morning, Frankie dressed for church, he'd almost lost his religion last night and needed the solace God could give. He'd prayed about the situation and felt led to stand his ground. He would see how she reacted this morning. He arrived at church as the first song ended. Lisbeth played the piano, and Victor directed the singing. The Douglas' gathered on their pew, he sat in the vacant space next to Ruthie. She glanced and smiled. He wanted to kiss her sweet lips.

He smiled in return. He craved the touch of her hand, but he would stay cool and see where she led him.

Pastor Lowe advanced to the entrance of the church to shake hands with people as they exited. Ruthie's friends peppered her with questions.

Frankie walked toward his friend. Victor shook his hand. "Good to see you at church today."

"I thought since it's almost Christmas, I better come."

"Join us for lunch at Uncle Walter's house. Aunt Delores always has more than enough."

"Thanks, I'd love to."

Frankie made his way to his car. He started toward Ruthie, but she gossiped with her friends. She raised her hand to wave goodbye. He hesitated and climbed in his Ford.

Ruth Ann climbed in the back seat of the car with Lisbeth and threw her purse in the floor.

Lisbeth reached for the handbag. "What's the matter with you?"

She grabbed the bag from her sister. "Nothing's the matter."

Lisbeth squinted her eyes. "So, Frankie sat with you this morning?"

"It was the only seat available."

"No, it wasn't. I can see everything from the piano, and he entered the church searching for someone. When he saw you, he headed straight for the pew, like you saved him a seat."

"I did not save him a seat."

"I saw how you smiled at each other."

Ruth Ann rolled her eyes and screeched. "Oh, for goodness sake, will you shut up."

Hattie faced the rear seat. "Girls, I'm not having this today. Ruth Ann's here two days and y'all are already fighting like cats. Stop. Now."

Jacob parked next to Victor's car.

Lisbeth spotted the Model A Ford. "Frankie's here."

Ruth Ann climbed from the back seat. "So?"

Lisbeth hurried to walk beside her sister. "So?" She dug her elbow in her sister's side. "I know you like him and he likes you. Admit it."

Ruth Ann pushed her sister and ran into the house.

Hattie and Dottie helped Delores put dinner on the table while Ruth Ann and Lisbeth held the babies.

Frankie watched Ruthie as she played with Carol Ann. He eased toward them, and Carol Ann stretched her arms.

She handed her over. "Here, she wants you. I'm glad you came for lunch. I watched you leave, and I thought you didn't want to see me."

He raised the tiny girl over his head. "She likes to be high so she can see everything." Frankie lowered the baby in his arms and winked at Ruth Ann. "After yesterday, you're all I've thought about."

"Yeah, me, too." She placed a kiss on the baby's cheek. "No, both of these kids love you."

"It's because I see them more than you do." Frankie inhaled a slow breath to steady his nerves. "Would you like to go to a movie with me this afternoon?"

"Is this a date?"

He smiled and lowered his voice. "Do you want it to be a date?"

"I don't know." She stared into his eyes. "Do

you?"

Frankie's stomach sunk in his belly, would she turn him down? "Let's say two good friends are going to see a movie together."

She put her hand on his arm. "It's a date... I mean its two good friends going to see a movie."

After lunch Ruth Ann dried dishes and placed them in the white hutch. "Ma, I'm going to the picture show with Frankie."

Hattie wrinkled her brow. "Did he ask you out on a date?"

"There's a movie I want to see. Frankie agreed to take me."

She put her thumb and index finger on Ruth Ann's chin and twisted her face toward her. "So now you're seeing two boys? What about Ronald? What would he say about this?"

She jerked her head from her mother's grasp. "What Ronald doesn't know won't hurt him." She headed toward the door.

Hattie called after her, "Ruth Douglas, come here."

She stopped. "What's the big deal?"

"When did you and Frankie become buddies?"

She ignored her mother, marched from the kitchen, and grabbed her purse off the table. "Frankie, I'm ready."

He said goodbye to everyone, hugged Delores, and thanked her for the delicious Sunday dinner. Ruthie waited in the passenger seat. He entered the car and glared. "You act like you're embarrassed to go out with me. You didn't tell anyone goodbye. What are you pouting about?"

"I got into it with Ma."

"What about?" Frankie started the car.

She searched her purse for lipstick. "Mother-daughter stuff. You know how she is."

He did know. It took a lot to ruffle Hattie's feathers, but when you did, she'd put you in your place. He eased the car down the road and headed to town. He couldn't believe his luck. Instead of sitting behind Ruthie watching her have fun with her other boyfriends, he would sit beside her, holding her hand.

They sat on the last row of the theater. The movie started, and Frankie put his arm around her. He loved the way she snuggled onto his shoulder. He watched her get lost in the picture. He concentrated on one thing. Her. Toward the end of the movie, he kissed her. She responded, and he wanted to cry out. It felt so good to have her close to him, kissing him. The lights glared, he stopped kissing her and removed his arm from around her shoulders. "Let's get a milkshake before I take you home."

Frankie parked in front of the Tastee Drive-In and waited for the car hop. "What flavor do you want?"

She studied the menu board. "What flavor are you getting?"

"Strawberry."

"Good. I'll get chocolate, and we can share."

Frankie grinned, *she always wants everything.* "Sounds like a good idea to me." He raised her hand to his lips.

The carhop sashayed over with the milkshakes, and Frankie payed him. He handed her his strawberry milkshake so she could get a taste before he gave her the chocolate. "How long are you going to be here?"

She smacked her lips. "The strawberry's delicious.

I'll be here two weeks."

He watched her enjoy the chocolate milkshake. "I hope we can do this every day while you're here."

"Don't you have to work?"

He realized he wouldn't get to taste the chocolate milkshake when he heard Ruthie's straw suck air. "Victor says we won't have to work on Christmas Eve, Christmas Day, and New Year's Day. We don't have too much work, so I'll have some afternoons off. Victor's having a New Year's Eve party at the hangar for our customers and some friends. Do you want to go with me?" Frankie handed the rest of his milkshake to her.

She finished the strawberry shake. "I've never gone to a New Year's Eve party. Ma always makes me go to the Watch Night Service at church."

He smiled as she finished off the shake. *God how I love to please you.* "With Victor and Dottie throwing the party, your mother shouldn't worry about you."

"They're at the church until after midnight anyway, who's keeping the babies?"

"Avery and Annie will stay at Victor's house with them. I know Dottie needs a break; those kids are a handful. Time to get you home. I'll call you tomorrow, and we'll do something when I get off work."

She handed him her empty glass. "Sounds like fun."

Chapter Eighteen

Frankie escorted Ruthie to the front door. She trudged ahead, and he made no moves to hold her hand. He wanted it to appear they were just friends returning from a movie. Sure enough, the curtain fluttered, Mrs. Douglas watched from the window. "I had a good time tonight," he said in a soft voice.

"I did too," Ruthie whispered. Will I see you tomorrow?"

"Yes." Frankie opened the screen door.

She grinned as she closed the wooden door. She glided upstairs and let out a sigh of relief that her mother didn't confront her. She opened a drawer and found her flannel gown and dressed for bed.

Lisbeth opened the door and barreled in. "So, you and Frankie, huh?"

She shifted her back to her sister to slide off her brassiere and tossed the gown over her head. "We saw a movie at the picture show, no big deal."

Lisbeth fell on the bed and gazed at the ceiling. "Oh, yeah, it's a big deal. You know you love him, and he's always been crazy about you. About time, I say. Although Ma's furious. She's been fussing all afternoon. Thinks you're leading two boys on. She's the one who liked Ronald, the rest of us not so much. Pa's pleased but he won't say one way or the other but I can tell. He even told Ma to mind her own business."

Ruth Ann sat on the bed. "He did? What'd she say then?"

"She made me leave the room, but I stood at the door and listened. She said you were her oldest daughter and she would not have you flitting around with two boys at a time and people talking about you like you were a whore."

"She said whore?" She stared at her sister, she'd never heard her mother say anything but 'John Brown' when she got mad.

"Yes, I tiptoed to my room, but I heard Pa yell, 'shut your mouth, Ruth Ann is not a whore.'"

"What happened then?" she whispered.

Lisbeth sat in the chair and pulled her legs under her. "I sat in my room reading when Ma came upstairs. I heard her crying, and she slammed the bedroom door. Pa proceeded to their room, and they made up. I played the piano so I wouldn't hear them. Ma fixed us supper and acted like nothing happened. I think she's having trouble accepting the fact her two girls are grown. Well, you are, and I almost am. I think she hoped you'd marry Ronald, and she wouldn't have to worry about you anymore."

Ruth Ann sat at her dressing table and brushed her hair. "I know what she's worried about. She thinks I'm going to get knocked up. I found their marriage certificate. Victor was born seven months after they got married, but don't tell her I told you. She doesn't know I know."

Lisbeth stood and put her hands on her hips. "You mean she and Pa? Before they were married? That explains everything. Since you left, she preaches the same sermon to me. Lisbeth, be a good girl, don't let the boys take advantage of you. Boy, you think you know your parents."

Ruth Ann jumped from her chair and pinched Lisbeth's arm.

Lisbeth slapped her hand away. "Ouch, that hurt."

She put her hand over Lisbeth's mouth. "You're talking too loud. You know Ma has ears like a bat. Please don't say anything to anyone. Victor has to know. But they've been married twenty-six years and love each other dearly."

Lisbeth nodded and rubbed her arm. "I know, now I understand Ma and why she worries."

"Ma and Pa loved each other, and they got married and had us. I admire them. I hope I'm as happy when I find the right one as they are."

Lisbeth walked to the door and turned to face her sister. "I think you've found the right one. You'll never find anyone who loves you more than Frankie does."

****

The next morning, Ruth Ann drove Jacob's car into town and headed to Price's Jewelry Store. She parked on Main Street in front of the drug store. She exited the car, and the cold wind cut through her light coat, she fastened the top button and stuffed her hands in the pockets. She glanced in the window of Hanson's Department Store and saw the perfect sweater for Lisbeth.

First, she would find something for Frankie. She entered Price's Jewelry Store and wandered to the men's section. She glanced at the tie clips and tie tacks until she found the perfect one. She chose a silver tie clip engraved with a biplane. Frankie spent Christmas Day with their family every year. This year the family would celebrate Christmas at Victor's house. She couldn't wait to surprise him with a present.

She entered the department store and bought the sweater for Lisbeth. Her shopping done, she decided to surprise Frankie at work and drove out of town to Andrews Field.

Frankie walked from the back of the hangar as she entered. "What brings you out here today?"

She sat at his desk. "I had to go to town and wanted to stop and see you while I was out." She picked up a piece of paper and admired the drawing of an airplane. "You're good, didn't know you could draw."

"It's just doodles. Glad you came by." He lowered his voice and gazed around the hangar. "Hey, you wanna do something tonight?"

"I do. The Christmas play's tonight. Lisbeth'll be mad if I don't go. She's playing all the music. Let's go together." She turned and admired some trophies on a small bookcase behind his desk. "Are these yours?"

"Yeah, got 'em at some contests I entered when I was a barnstormer." Frankie leaned on his desk. "I heard Victor say Jack Andrew will portray the baby Jesus. Ought to be interesting, I know he won't stay in the manger. How 'bout I pick you up at seven?"

She stood and moved closer. A movement caught her eye, Al stared at them from the corner of the hangar. "See you tonight." She touched his cheek.

He followed her to the door and watched as she got in the car and drove off. "You can come out now Al, she's gone."

Al appeared from the shadows grinning from ear to ear. "Finally, you two are getting along. When did this start?"

"I took her to a movie yesterday's all."

"I sense more than a movie. When did this flighty little thing start comin' 'round?"

Frankie guided Al toward the front of the hangar and lowered his voice all the while making sure Victor stayed in his office. "I'm seeing Ruthie while she's home. I don't care who knows, but I don't want to cause any trouble with my job. The Douglas' are a close family, and I don't want any of them thinking I'm taking advantage. She came on to me Saturday when I flew her home from Atlanta."

Al grabbed Frankie's arm. "Came on to you. Whatcha mean?"

Frankie whispered, "I mean, if I wasn't a gentleman, she would no longer be a lady. I drove her home before anything happened. Then I went to the bar, had a few drinks. After some alcohol and prayer, I decided to follow where she led me, and this is where we are. I'm taking her to the church Christmas play tonight, and she's my date for the New Year's Eve party."

"Son, didn't I tell you?" Al's voice grew louder. "The girl's in love with ya."

Frankie grabbed his arm. "Quiet. Victor's going to hear you. I'm not going to get my hopes up,. She has go to school, and she'll see the dandy every day, she'll forget about me." Frankie shuffled toward his desk.

"If Ruthie loves you, she'll come back to you when school's over. If she don't, she ain't worth it anyway." Al followed him.

Frankie glanced toward Victor's office. "I know, don't say anything about Saturday night to Victor."

"My lips are sealed son, very pleased to see you

happy."

Chapter Nineteen

Christmas morning, Frankie wrapped Ruthie's present in brown paper and tied it with a red ribbon. He hadn't had a girlfriend at Christmas in years. He arrived at Victor's house early so he could watch the babies while Victor and Dottie got things ready. He put the babies on a blanket on the floor and played blocks with them.

Victor sat in a chair and watched. "They love you, you know."

"I love them, too. You've got some sweet kids."

"I want them to call you Uncle Frankie if you don't mind. You're like my brother anyway."

"I'd be honored." He stacked blocks, and Jack Andrew shoved them over and laughed.

Victor sat on the edge of the couch. "Hey man, what's going on with you and Ruth Ann?"

He left Jack Andrew and Carol Ann and sat in the chair. "I wondered how long it would take you to say something."

Victor smiled at his friend. "I know you've carried a torch for her a long time. I know she hasn't been nice to you. She gave us both hell when she was in high school. I always thought she cared about you but was too stubborn and bull headed to tell you. I don't want her to hurt you. I know how she can be."

Carol Ann crawled to Frankie's chair, and he put

her in his lap. "I like the new Ruthie, and I've decided to enjoy this while I can."

"You know she'll be going to school next week." Victor grabbed his son and glided him through the air. The baby stretched out his arms and laughed.

"Don't remind me." Frankie bounced the baby on his knee.

"I'm concerned. This year's been hard for you." Victor placed Jack Andrew on the quilt and gave him a block.

"I'll be all right, no matter what happens."

Soon the house filled with family and friends, talking and laughing. The smell of baked ham and yeast rolls mingled with the smell of the bourbon from Aunt Delores' fruit cake. After everyone finished Christmas dinner, Victor handed out presents.

Frankie pulled Ruthie's from his pocket. "Merry Christmas."

She put the box to her ear and shook. "What is it?"

"Open and see."

She tore open the paper and lifted the lid on the little box. "Oh, Frankie, how beautiful."

He removed the necklace from the box and fastened the clasp behind her neck. "Mr. Price suggested it since garnet is the birthstone for January. I hope you like it."

She put her hand on the necklace and traced the heart with her fingers. "I love it."

"I hope you think of me when you wear it, you've had my real heart for a long time."

She opened her purse and retrieved his present. "Merry Christmas."

He stared at the small box wrapped in paper with a

Christmas tree design and tied with a gold ribbon. "You got me a present."

"Of course."

His heart swelled in his chest. He didn't get many presents and one from Ruthie was special. He took his time opening the box using his pocket knife to cut the adhesive tape. "The JN-Four. Where'd you find this?"

"Price's Jewelry Store, same place you found my necklace. I'm surprised you didn't see it."

"I had my mind on your gift. Thank you. This is special." Frankie wrapped the paper around the box and placed it in his pocket along with the gold ribbon. He watched the others open their presents and thanked God for his adopted family. Carol Ann got a baby doll and Jack Andrew a wooden airplane. The girl abandoned her doll and wanted the plane.

Dottie scooped her baby girl and grabbed the doll. "Let's rock your doll to sleep." She cradled her daughter in her arms and made her way to the quiet of the bedroom.

Frankie grabbed the boy and lifted him so Jack Andrew could hold the plane in the air. He couldn't remember a better Christmas. Surrounded by people who loved him and treated him like family made him happy, but Christmas with Ruthie and her attention put the icing on the cake. He wouldn't think about her in Atlanta with the dandy. He'd enjoy each and every day he had with her and would worry about the rest later.

Chapter Twenty

Ruth Ann spent her day avoiding her mother. She didn't want to listen to Hattie harp that Ronald had more to offer than Frankie. She liked Ronald and Frankie, why'd she have to choose? She didn't want to get married, she wanted to have fun. The earth tumbling from under her when Frankie kissed her was a surprise. With Ronald, she struggled to keep him at a distance while Frankie acted like a perfect gentleman. She ached to have Frankie touch her in the places no one had before, but since their first kiss and her realization of what could happen between them, she appreciated his approach. She recognized how hard dating her must be when he was used to making love to a woman and now had to restrain himself. If he asked her or even seduced her, she'd let him. She spent most of her days dreaming about the very thing.

She sat at her dressing table putting on her new necklace when her mother marched in without knocking. "Going out with Frankie again?"

She dabbed Arpège perfume behind her ear. "Yes, we're going to a movie."

Hattie spat her words like a fire cracker. "I like Frankie, he's like a brother to Victor but you never liked him. You always called him white trash, and now you're slipping out with him every chance you get. I don't like this one bit. You better not be going to his house."

She glared at Hattie, rage roared through her. She wanted to slap her mother. "I don't appreciate what you're insinuating, I'm grown, and I'm going to make my own decisions. You raised me to be a good person. I know I was cruel to Frankie and Victor, too. I'm not proud of my actions, but lately I find I like Frankie's company. Now, if you'll excuse me, he's here."

Hattie grabbed her arm.

She leered at her mother. "I love you, Ma, but you're going to have to accept I'm grown now. I'll decide who I see and where I go, you have to trust me."

Hattie let go and started to cry. "I'm sorry. I don't want you to make a mistake. A woman's good name is all she has."

She placed her hand on her mother's arm. "I know, Ma. I'll be fine." She made her way down the steps toward the parlor where Frankie discussed Lisbeth's flying lessons with her father. "Yes, she's a natural, like her brother."

Jacob nodded. "Of course, she is. How many more lessons will she need?"

"Forty hours of flight instruction are required before she solos. We could give her two lessons a week instead of one. She'd be done in half the time."

"I'll give that some consideration." Jacob stood. "You two have fun tonight."

Frankie guided her to the car. "Is there a problem?"

She sat in the car. "Everything's fine."

He climbed behind the wheel. "Doesn't appear fine to me, tell me what's wrong."

She glanced at the house where her mother stared out of her bedroom window. "Ma gave me a hard time.

She can't understand us going out together. She keeps reminding me of how bad I treated you. She gives me the impression she thinks we're doing something we shouldn't. She even made me promise I wouldn't go to your house."

Frankie backed his car to the street, pushed in the clutch and placed the car in first gear. "Your mother doesn't like you dating a man who's been married before. She thinks I'm going to take advantage of you."

She scooted over in the bench seat. "Well, are you?"

He smiled and put his arm around her. "Don't tempt me."

She kissed him on the cheek. "I can't believe I'm here with you and we're on a date."

"Yes, imagine, me and you on a date." He parked the car on the street in front of the movie house.

They sat on the back row. Frankie kept the kissing light. Reining in his desire for Ruthie became harder and harder. He craved her. He wanted her sweet body naked under him, but he wanted to love her, protect her, and spend the rest of his life with her. He never felt this way about any woman, even Audrey.

After the movie, he drove her straight home. "How about going with me to a dance at the community center tomorrow night?"

She jumped in her seat. "Sounds like a lot of fun. I love to dance."

He enveloped her hands in his. "I know you do. I remember seeing you dance around your house when I visited Victor."

"And you still want to be seen with me?"

"I sure do. We can practice our dancing for the

New Year's Eve party." He opened the door and helped her out of her seat.

She noticed the silhouette of her mother in the window. "Ma's watching us."

"I know." He led her up the steps. "I'll be here at seven tomorrow evening."

She gazed into his eyes and smiled. "Can't wait."

Chapter Twenty-One

Frankie buttoned his red striped shirt and tucked it in his pants. He took extra care tying his red tie with a diamond design and attached his new tie clip. The gift reminded him of the Jenny and his precious Ruthie. Two things he cherished.

He arrived at Ruthie's house and Hattie met him at the door. "Good evening Mrs. Douglas."

"Come in, Ruth Ann'll be here in a minute."

He took the opportunity to set the record straight with Ruthie's mother. "Mrs. Douglas, you don't have to worry about me taking advantage of your daughter."

She crossed her arms and unsettled him with a hardened glare. "I don't like this, but it appears Ruth Ann's made up her mind."

"You don't have to explain. I know I'm not the type of man you wanted your daughter to date. I'm taking her to the dance, then we'll come straight home. You have my word."

"If you want to see her again this week, you'll do that."

Ruth Ann eased down the stairs. "See you later, Ma."

He started the car, and when they were out of eye sight, she scooted to the middle of the seat. "I heard part of your conversation. I'm sorry she gave you a hard time."

"I told her the truth. I'll never take advantage of you, no matter how much I want to."

She rubbed her hand over his cheek. "You want to take advantage of me?"

He loved the feel of her soft fingers on his skin. He half closed his eyes and memorized her touch. "No, I want to do things to you, but I wouldn't call it taking advantage of you. Believe me, you'll like it."

"If it's anything like our first kiss, I'm sure I will."

He put his hand on her back and led her into the community center. Balloons and streamers hung from the ceiling. A small orchestra had their instruments set and ready to play. He noticed the two punch bowls and guided Ruthie toward the one without alcohol. He poured a cup for her. "This is the punch bowl we'll drink from tonight. Do not drink from the other bowl."

She raised the glass to her nose and sniffed. "What's wrong with the other bowl?"

He couldn't believe how naïve she was. "Is this your first dance here?"

"Yes. Ma never allowed me to go to a dance."

"The other one has whiskey mixed in, and I'll be damned if I'm taking you home spifficated."

She drained her cup of punch and placed the cup on the table. "Why not?" She rubbed her body against his arm and tiptoed, trying to reach his ear so no one could hear. "Easier for you to take advantage of me."

He bent and whispered. "If I ever, you know, take advantage of you, I want you to remember every moment." He refilled her cup.

They finished their drink and placed the cups on a tray. He put his hand on her back and led her to the dance floor. The orchestra played an upbeat number with the clarinet blaring the melody. Frankie pulled her in his arms and held her close while their feet moved to the music. He'd never had a better shag dance partner. She knew just when he was about to twirl her or push her away so their kicking legs wouldn't get tangled. She jumped in the air, and he caught her and spun around with her in his arms. He released her, her body slinking down his until her feet touched the floor. He drew her close as the music changed to a slow number. The feel of her breasts rising and falling against his chest pulsed in his core. His trousers tightened with his erection. He sang along with the band leader to "The Shadow Waltz" to take his mind off his arousal. When he got to the part, "Let me feel that I mean everything to you," he bent his head and kissed her.

When the song ended, she said, "I didn't know you could sing. You have a beautiful voice."

Frankie's gaze drifted to her lips stained with red lipstick. He longed to kiss her until the red disappeared into juicy, healthy pink lips. He licked his lips and sucked his bottom lip into his mouth. He gave her a wicked smile. "There's lots of things you don't know about me, Ruthie. I hope I have a chance to show you all of them."

"I hope you do, too." She gazed around the room. "I need to sit a moment."

He guided her to a chair and made his way to the punch table.

Several girls approached him, but each time he smiled and pointed to his date. They drank their punch and listened to the music. "Let's drink this and head home. The dance isn't over until midnight, but I want to get you home early."

She gulped her punch and handed him the cup. "Are you trying to make points with my mother?"

"Yes, reckon I am. Gonna see you every day before you leave, if I can."

"That would be swell." She put her arm through his, and they left the community center.

He escorted her to the door and spotted Hattie peering out the window. "I'll see you tomorrow. I had a great time."

"Don't I get a kiss goodnight?"

"Not with Mrs. Douglas watching." He stopped Ruthie from turning her head. "Don't. Trust me, she's watching."

She rolled her eyes. "Okay, but you owe me a kiss. I had a great time. Thanks, Frankie."

Chapter Twenty-Two

Ruth Ann chose a pink sweater and a gray wool skirt and placed them on the bed. She sat in her chair, her vacation would be over soon, and she'd return to school. She hadn't thought about Ronald, but her mother talked about him non-stop. He was the intellectual, and they had a lot in common. She could marry him and live the life she'd dreamed, married to a handsome actor, both of them performing on the New York stage.

Frankie was smart in a way Ronald would never be. He wouldn't let anyone run over him or anyone he loved. She felt safe with him, safe and loved. Ronald and his kisses and fondling never made her feel like Frankie did. She could practically see love coming from his pores. His emotions were sincere; he loved her and had for a long time. She didn't want to hurt him, but she had to be sure. The next few months in Atlanta would give her time to decide.

She heard the knock on the door and walked down the stairs.

Frankie stood at the door holding a corsage. "This is for you."

She took the pink carnation and pinned it to her sweater. "How'd you know what color I was wearing?"

"Just a lucky guess." He saw Hattie standing off to the side. "Happy New Year, Mrs. Douglas. I'll bring her home as soon as the party's over."

Hattie folder her arms. "See that you do."

She put her arm through Frankie's, and they entered the hangar. She gazed around amazed at the transformation. Frankie, Victor, and Al cleaned the space and placed chairs around the walls and left room in the middle for a dance floor. Victor settled his large radio from home in a corner. A punch and food table lined the back wall. About thirty people milled around. Al and Ethel met people at the door as they removed their coats and placed them in Victor's office. She handed her coat to Al. "Thanks, Mr. Gregory."

"Call me Al. I'm glad to see you and Frankie together. You've played quite a game of cat and mouse."

She opened her mouth but couldn't think of anything to say.

Al continued, "Frankie's a tough nut to crack, I know he loves you, but he may not tell you. Pride, you know."

"We're just dating."

Al chuckled and gave her a knowing look. "Is that what it is? You be careful. I don't wanna see my boy hurt. You're returning to the big city, but he'll be here waitin'. You remember that."

A wave of nausea rose from her stomach. Al was right; she didn't have a clue what she did to Frankie. "I won't forget."

"Good, now you have fun tonight."

She found Victor and Dottie. "Lots of people here. This is going to be fun."

Victor placed his arm around his wife and kissed the top of her head. "Yes, we're going to dance and ring in the New Year with a champagne toast at midnight. Ever had champagne?"

She'd never tasted wine. "No, I haven't."

He studied his sister. "I figured you used to drink with your friends in high school."

She remembered the hard time she gave her brother. "I wasn't as wild as you thought."

Victor placed Dottie so her back was against his chest and hugged her around the waist. "Good, I'm glad. The champagne is sparkly and cold. Don't drink too much. Ma will never let me hear the end of it. I'm glad to see you and Frankie getting along."

Frankie grabbed her hand. "Dance with me, they're playing 'The Shadow Waltz.'"

The slow song seduced everyone to the dance floor. He sang every word. When the song ended, he drew her close and kissed her. She smelled bourbon on his breath. "Have you been drinking?"

"Victor and I had a little drink to celebrate our success this year. Don't worry. I'm not drunk, nor will I be. I'm on my best behavior tonight. This is the first New Year's Eve that didn't involve alcohol since I was sixteen years old."

She loved his honesty. He was real and genuine and smelled like a man, not like lavender and Pond's Cream like Ronald.

He guided her to the food table. "Let's have some punch and a sandwich."

"Is the punch spiked?"

Frankie shook his head. "No, Victor won't allow it. But if you notice, some people have their own flask."

She watched Al pour something in his and Ethel's punch. "Does Ethel know Al put something in her punch?"

"It's a game with them. She acts like she doesn't want it, and he acts like he didn't do it. He puts a few drops each time, more in his than hers."

Al put his cup on the table and grabbed Ethel. They were playing "Ain't She Sweet" on the radio. He and Ethel commanded the dance floor with the Charleston.

Ruth Ann couldn't take her eyes off the pair. "Wow, they can shake a leg."

Frankie stared at his pal. "Yes, his favorite dance. I'm glad he's having a good time."

She studied Frankie, the admiration he had for the old man evident on his face. "You love him, don't you?"

"Yes, he and Victor are my best friends. Al's the father I never had."

She felt disgusted with herself. She'd never considered Frankie's feelings and how he suffered when his mother died and his father left town. She wondered how he could forgive her for the things she said, calling him white trash and stupid. "Frankie, I know I wasn't nice to you. I'm sorry for the hard time I gave you. I had a family and lived in a nice house in town. I didn't realize how hard your life was. Please forgive me."

He pulled her close giving her a deep kiss. He realized where he was when he heard Victor clear his throat. He stepped back, heat rising to his face. "Forgiven, let's dance."

A little before midnight, Frankie and Victor opened champagne bottles while she assisted Dottie with the glasses. The disc jockey at the radio station started the countdown. Everyone shouted the seconds, eager to toast the New Year. When the hour of midnight arrived, Frankie kissed her. She stood on her tiptoes and wrapped her arms around his neck.

Victor patted Frankie on the back and yelled, "Happy New Year, everyone." She stopped kissing him and glanced at her brother.

Victor shook Frankie's hand and smiled like a Cheshire cat. "I think nineteen thirty-seven will be your best year, old friend."

Frankie hugged Victor. "I hope so, man."

Al grabbed Frankie and gave him a bear hug, as much as he could. Frankie stood several inches taller. "Happy New Year, son."

"Happy New Year, Al."

Victor and Al gave her a kiss on the cheek and wished her a Happy New Year.

She watched as friends and customers toasted Frankie and Victor. She never dreamed they had such a good business and all these friends. Pride filled her heart. Frankie struggled from a famous barnstormer to a mill hand, then to a successful pilot and mechanic. Her brother struggled with their father. He didn't want Victor to fly and hoped flying in the United States Army Air Corps would be enough, but he proved his father wrong. They were very smart men, and she couldn't be prouder of them.

Chapter Twenty-Three

Frankie stared at his beautiful date. Excitement bubbled in his belly. He'd planned their detour home, down to the minute. He glanced at his pocket watch, it was time. He told Victor and Al he would join them later in the day to clean the hangar. He retrieved Ruthie's coat from Victor's office.

Ruthie helped Dottie collect glasses. Frankie whispered in her ear, "We've got to go. I need to get you home."

She continued to gather glasses. "We have plenty of time."

He took the glasses and placed them on the table and gave her a sly smile. "I have a stop to make. It won't take long, but we need to leave now."

He maneuvered his car through the old country road and turned onto a gravel side road. He parked so anyone traveling on the main road wouldn't see his car.

She glanced around. "Where are we going?"

He cut the engine. "I wanted to be alone with you for a few minutes. You'll be leaving Saturday, and I won't have a chance to do this." Frankie scooted over in the middle of the seat and placed Ruthie in his lap. He kissed her like a man starving for water.

She relaxed in his arms. He tugged her jacket off while he kissed her and threw it behind his seat. She placed his hand on her breast.

Frankie accepted her invitation. He kissed her on the neck while he raised her sweater and unfastened her brassiere. Her breast fell into his hand. He yanked her sweater over her head and kissed her delicate skin. He sucked her taut nipple into his mouth. She arched her back giving her body to him to do as he wanted.

She asked in a guttural whisper, "Frankie?"

He replaced his mouth with his thumb. "Yes, angel."

Her chest rose as she gasped for air. "I...I like that."

He groaned wanting much more than he'd ever taken from a woman. His heart beat faster supplying the blood demanded by his aching shaft. He reminded himself this night belonged to his beloved. He ignored his needs and turned his attention to pleasing his girl. Her breasts were smooth and heavy in his hand. He took his time savoring the smell, taste, and feel of each. He encircled the nipple sucking it into his mouth. He continued memorizing each breast amazed at the softness.

She fidgeted in his lap. "Frankie." Her voice soft, pleading, breathless. "I want your skin on my skin."

He placed her so she straddled him and kissed her.

She unbuttoned his shirt and settled her bare flesh against his. Her hungry kiss and the feel of her bubs against his chest teased and tormented him. "Holy shit, Ruthie, you're killing me." He reached for her brassiere and pushed her away trying to fit her arms in the straps. He'd gone as far as he could without branding her with his throbbing erection.

She cooed, "Don't stop." She continued to kiss him and sucked his bottom lip.

He gave in and threw her underwear on the floor. He groaned, consumed by need, not for him but a need to please...her. He'd always put his desires above anyone, but now, seeing his angel happy was all that mattered.

He positioned her in his lap and kissed her while he teased her nipples with his fingers. He nuzzled her neck. She smelled like a bouquet of flowers. He closed his eyes and inhaled. He smelled roses and lilac.

She reclaimed his lips, in a demanding and urgent kiss.

He put his hand under her skirt and traced her thigh above her stockings. His fingers caressed her silky flesh. He broke the kiss and leaned his head on the car seat. "Your skin is so soft." He kept his hand on the tender spot of her thigh and debated whether to continue to the target he craved or keep touching her delicate skin.

She cupped his head in her hands and placed her lips on his. She kissed him like she could crawl into his body. No woman had ever kissed him like this. He stopped kissing her, his eyes raked over her petite body curled in his lap. His finger found the target and entered the tight depths of her. He groaned. "My God, Ruthie." She was so ready. He couldn't give her everything now, but he prayed someday he would, tonight it was all about her.

She arched her back and at the same time the look on her face begged to know what he planned to do.

He continued exploring. "It's all right, precious. I'm not going to hurt you, relax. Remember when I told you, I could do things to you and you'd like it."

She nodded her head and closed her eyes.

He watched her. She teetered at the edge of the precipice, the desire to please her gave him more enjoyment than he'd had with dozens of women. He continued his exploration, sealing to his memory the moves that pleased her. She relinquished control to him, he watched as wave after wave of ecstasy took her. When she cried out, a tear escaped his eye.

She draped her body around his. He felt like he would explode as she tantalized him with her kisses and sweet moans. She unfastened his belt and the button of his pants. She placed both her hands on his face and guided his lips to hers.

He relaxed against the seat and lost his mind in her kiss. Blood pumped, heating his body with warmth leaving a throbbing ache in his groin. He struggled, his need of her at war with what was right. His arms pushed her away and pulled her toward him at the same time. He nudged her aside and fastened his pants, then his belt. "Precious, we have to stop. I can't."

"You can. I want you." Her hands were inside his shirt, her fingers raked through the hair on his chest. "Please." She tilted her head and pushed her lips into a pout.

He stared wanting to suck her lips into his mouth. The bulge in his pants reminding him they weren't finished. For the first time in his life, he did the right thing. He straightened in the seat and placed her beside him. "I've got to get you home." He fumbled with the clasp on her brassiere until they were secured, then pulled her sweater over her head.

She searched for words. "Frankie, that was, I mean I'm kind of embarrassed. I've never, well you know. I don't know very much…"

Frankie pulled her hand to his lips and kissed it never taking his eyes from hers. "Did you like the way I made you feel?"

Her eyes bore into his soul. "Yes," she said in a breathy whisper.

He wanted to tell her what he did was love her like he'd never loved anyone before. He wanted to say the three words he'd never said to anyone. He wanted time to stand still. "Well, then, nothing to be embarrassed about is there?" He searched behind his seat for her coat. "Put this on before you catch cold. Ruthie, I." He hesitated and kissed the top of her head.

She pivoted. "Yes?"

He gazed into her eyes, *I'm a coward.* "I. I'll miss you."

She whispered and closed her eyes. "I'll miss you, too."

He smoothed his hand over her hair. "You'd better comb your hair and put on some lipstick so your lips match the glow in your cheeks. We don't want your mother getting suspicious."

She grabbed her purse and took out her comb as Frankie clicked the inside light.

He started the car, backed around and headed to town. "Do you want me to fly you to Atlanta Saturday?"

"Will you?" She snapped her purse closed.

"I'd be happy to."

"How about my play in March?" She stared into the dark night, "I won't be home before then. We have rehearsals every weekend."

"I'll be there," Frankie assured her.

She put her hand on his leg. "Promise?"

"Promise." Frankie lifted her hand and kissed it.

He parked in front of the Douglas house with a few minutes to spare. "Home, safe and sound."

He opened Ruthie's door and helped her out. He watched the curtain in the parlor flutter. He opened the screen door and stepped aside. "We'll go to a movie tomorrow night, if you want."

She didn't step any closer. "Yes."

Frankie walked to his car, he opened the door and stared. Ruthie stood under the porch light holding the handle of the screen door. He raised his hand to wave and climbed in his car and inhaled the scent of Ruthie mingling with her perfume.

Chapter Twenty-Four

Hattie met her daughter at the door. "Did you have a good time?"

Ruth Ann hung her coat on the peg. "I had a wonderful time. I had no idea that Victor and Frankie had so many friends."

"Yes, they have a good business. I'm proud of both of them. If you hadn't been so mean and thought of anyone but yourself, you would have noticed before now."

She hugged her mother. "Happy New Year, Ma. I'm going to bed."

She undressed and stood in front of the mirror staring at her naked body. She'd never let a boy do what Frankie did to her tonight. What she felt, what they did, well, it was better than what she dreamed it would be. She pulled her gown over her head and sat at her dressing table. *How will I make it through the next few months without Frankie?* She combed her hair, lost in thought, lost in the certainty of Frankie's love, lost in the joy she'd saved her body for the barnstormer.

****

Ruth Ann's suitcases lay open on her bed. She admired the new clothes she received for Christmas as she folded and placed them in the suitcase. She counted the hours until she'd be with Frankie. He would pick her up at noon to fly her to Atlanta. She heard a knock on the front door. She glanced at the clock, ten in the morning, too early for Frankie. She stood at the stairs and listened. *Ronald? What is he doing here?* She tiptoed to her room and prayed he'd go away.

Hattie raced upstairs to her bedroom and closed the door. "Ronald's here to take you to school."

She sat at her dressing table and combed her hair. "He's not supposed to be here. Frankie's flying me to Atlanta this afternoon."

"Ronald wanted to surprise you. He drove out of his way to come here and get you, and you're going."

"I am not. Tell him I'm not here." She dabbed perfume behind her ear.

"Oh, you're going. He's a nice boy and has a lot to offer you. Don't mess this up." She threw clothes in the suitcase.

"Mess what up? You think every boy I date, I have to marry. I'll marry the person I choose."

Hattie put her hand on Ruth Ann's arm to settle her. "I've kept my mouth shut this week because I knew you were leaving, but you're making a big mistake. I think the world of Frankie, but he's not the one for you."

She jerked her arm away. "Frankie's right. He said you didn't want me to see him because he had lived with Audrey as man and wife, but I'll tell you this, he's more of a gentleman than Ronald. So think about that while we're alone in Atlanta."

Her mother sat on the bed and cried.

She wadded up clothes and threw them in her suitcase. "You raised me to be a good person. Leave me alone and let me live my life."

Hattie dried the tears on her face with a

handkerchief. "My mother raised me right, but I made some terrible mistakes I don't want you to make."

She gave her mother her full attention. "What mistakes?"

She stood. "Nothing that concerns you. I expect you downstairs in ten minutes. You are riding to Atlanta with Ronald. I'll tell Frankie when he gets here."

How dare Ronald come here and assume I want him to drive me to Atlanta. She removed a piece of paper from her desk and scribbled a note.

Frankie,

I didn't know Ronald planned to take me to Atlanta. He arrived this morning, and Ma made me go. I'm glad you're coming to my play in March. I'll miss you every day.

XXXOOO's

Ruth Ann

Hattie knocked on her bedroom door. "Ruth Ann, time to go. Ronald's waiting."

She opened the door. "Please give this note to Frankie when he comes."

Her mother dropped the note in her apron pocket. "I'll help you with your suitcases."

Ronald ran to meet her and took a suitcase from Mrs. Douglas. "Ruth Ann, I've missed you. I wanted to surprise you."

"You surprised me." She gave her mother a curt goodbye and headed out the door.

Ronald turned the car toward Atlanta. "Did you have a nice Christmas?"

"I had a nice Christmas, how about you?" She added under her breath, "The best I ever had."

"I enjoyed the holidays, but I missed you so much. I couldn't wait for the vacation to be over. I had to see you."

Once they got on the main road headed to Atlanta, she settled in her seat and closed her eyes. She would pretend to be asleep so he wouldn't talk. Her breakfast sat heavy in her stomach mingling with the dread of Frankie learning that she was with Ronald.

She didn't stir until the car stopped in front of her building. Ronald retrieved her suitcases while she opened her front door.

He placed the bags in the bedroom, strolled into the sitting room, and placed a small box wrapped in Christmas paper in her hand. "Merry Christmas."

The present, light as a feather, felt heavy in her hand. "I didn't get you anything."

He waited for her to open the gift. "No problem, I wanted you to have this."

She tore the paper off and opened the box. *A cameo ring, he bought me a ring.* "Lovely, thank you."

He tugged the ring from the box and put it on her finger. "I hope someday to get you a diamond."

"What do you mean a diamond? This doesn't mean..." She stared waiting for a response.

He pulled her in his arms and kissed her. "No, I'm not asking you to marry me...yet. I wanted to buy something for my best girl."

Best girl? She didn't want to hurt him, but after her time with Frankie, she wouldn't commit to anything. "Thank you, you are so sweet to think of me. I'm very sorry I didn't get you anything."

He guided her to the sitting area. "Tell me about your holiday."

Her thoughts drifted to Frankie. He would be furious if he knew she was alone with Ronald. "This was my best Christmas, ever."

He brushed her hair out of her face and kissed her. "What made this year the best?"

She scooted away from him. "I spent time with my family, and I attended a dance in town and my first New Year's Eve party. Victor and uh, Dottie had the party in the hangar and invited their friends and customers. I had a glass of champagne."

"I gathered with friends, and we celebrated New Year's Eve together. We had champagne, too. Only thing missing was you."

She didn't want to lie or hurt his feelings. "Sounds like we both had a nice Christmas and New Year. I can't wait to start work on the play. Did you rehearse any while you were off?"

He put his arm around her shoulder. "No, did you?"

She laughed and shook her head. "I didn't either."

Ronald gathered her in his arms while his lips searched hers. He moved his hands along her body. A surge of emptiness filled her gut. With Frankie she felt loved, but with Ronald she felt dirty and ashamed. She placed her hands on his cheeks and stared. Desire emanated from his green eyes. She had to stop. "I'm tired, and I need to get organized for school. Thanks for the ring and driving me."

Ronald ran his index finger down her nose and smiled. "I'm tired, too. See you in the morning, beautiful."

After Ronald left, she sat and relived every single moment she spent with Frankie. She started at the beginning when she attempted to seduce him to the last night when they went to the picture show. She prayed he understood when her mother gave him the note. He had to know she had no choice but to go with Ronald. The next couple of months away from him would be torture but Frankie promised he would see her play and she would put on her best performance.

Chapter Twenty-Five

Frankie showered and shaved and put on his best blue jeans and shirt. He grabbed his leather jacket and drove to Ruthie's house. He loved her more than his own life. The last two weeks gave him hope for a future with her. He parked in the gravel drive and made his way to the house.

Hattie opened the door and met him on the porch. "Ruth Ann's already gone to Atlanta. I'm sorry you drove over for nothing."

He peered inside the house, expecting to see Ruthie. "What do you mean, gone? Did Victor take her?"

She closed the door and crossed her arms against the cold. "No, Ronald stopped by this morning to get her. She's gone."

"Gone, did she say anything about me? We made plans for me to fly her."

She shivered from the cold. "No, she didn't say anything. I'm freezing. I'm going in the house. Sorry for your trouble, Frankie."

He stomped to his car. *What the hell? The bitch used me. Same old Ruthie, wanting to have a good time. Did she seduce me and lead me on to practice for one of her plays? How could I be so stupid? First Audrey and now Ruthie, what a fool.*

He angled his car toward the tavern. He wanted to

get drunk and forget what happened this week. He could still taste Ruthie and the smell of her perfume lingered in his car.

He settled at a table with a pitcher of beer. He gulped down the first glass and poured another. He wanted to believe in Ruthie. The way she kissed him and allowed him to love her proved she had feelings for him. Didn't it? He should have told her he loved her. Stake his claim. Taken her to the justice of the peace and married her before she had time to leave him. Actions speak louder than words, and she left with the dandy. No call. No goodbye. No kiss my ass.

Several women joined him throughout the afternoon, but they didn't stay. He bought them drinks and smiled as they flirted. As the day wore on, he switched from beer to whiskey. When the ladies discovered he wouldn't take them home with him, they left his table. Frankie stood to leave. He weaved to the door knocking over chairs. He reached for the door handle of the car. He stumbled and fell. A man helped him to his feet. He left his car and wandered home.

Deputy Riley's police car rolled down the street. Frankie slowed as the car headed his way.

Shit, this is all I need right now.

Adam Riley stopped. He got out and leaned on the top of the car. "That you, Frankie?"

"Yeah."

"Need a ride?"

"Nope." He stumbled over a crack in the sidewalk.

"Are you drunk?"

"As a matter of fact, Mr. Deputy Adam, jerk face, Riley, I am splifficated."

Adam leapt around the car and opened the door.

"Get in."

Frankie ignored him. "You ain't arrestin' me. I done nothin'."

"Not arresting you, taking you home. Get your ass in this car."

He squinted and tried to focus on the man. "What the hell? Sure, take me home."

Adam opened the back door of the police car.

He glared at the deputy and stumbled into the seat.

The lawman turned the car around and headed toward the drunk's street.

Frankie's head bobbled, his body followed as he slid on the seat.

Adam peered in his mirror. "Frankie, sit."

He jerked his body straight. "Who the hell are you?"

"You're in a police car. I'm taking you home."

He stared at Adam bidding his eyes to focus. "Jerk face, yeah, thanks, man."

"Deputy Riley to you." Adam said with authority.

Frankie slurred his words. "Yep, Deputy Riley. You were always a little man who wanted to bully people. I beat your ass in the fifth grade."

"You beat my ass in the ninth grade, too." The deputy stared into the rear view mirror, a look of disgust on his face.

He put his head in his hands. "I did, I did. I'm sorry, didn't mean to hurt you. Did I hurt you?

"Yeah, you did." Adam turned the car onto Frankie's street.

"Now, you got a badge and car. Important man, still a jerk face, though."

Adam stopped the car in front of Frankie's house.

"You're home. Need any help?"

"No, man." Frankie ran his hand over the door until he found the handle. "I got it. I got it. Thanks, sorry, thanks, man.

He stumbled on the front steps and grabbed the rail to steady himself. He searched his pocket for his keys, but they tumbled out of his grasp. He got on his hands and knees searching. He found them, still on his knees he inserted the key into the lock. He crawled in the door and climbed to standing holding to the wall before he slammed the front door. He spun around several times until he focused on the door to his bedroom. He placed his hand on the wall for support as he weaved his way to the bed.

He woke to a blinding light shining in the window. His head felt like someone had a hammer pounding on it. He jumped out of bed and raced to the toilet. After getting rid of everything in his stomach, he soaked a wash rag with cold water and rubbed his face and neck. He needed coffee and stumbled to his kitchen. He ground the coffee beans and opened the drawer to scoop the grounds. He fumbled with the percolator spilling grounds on the counter. "Son of a bitch." He sat in a chair and held his head in his hands. "What the hell did I think I was doing with Ruthie. Son of a bitch."

Frankie had to get sober and fly. He needed the sky more than he'd ever needed it in his life. He bathed, put on clean clothes, and trudged to the bar to get his car.

Mr. Andrews helped him ready the Jenny and prop it off. He took off and did a lazy eight and waved to Mr. Andrews. He headed in the direction of Atlanta. *What the hell am I doing? I don't even know where she lives.*

He continued flying, and soon, he arrived at

Candler Field. He landed the Jenny and went to the restaurant. He sat in a booth and ordered a sandwich. The airport buzzed with activity. He enjoyed watching people come and go. He made two decisions. He would not run after Ruthie like a dog in heat, and he'd never let anyone make him mad enough to drink like he did yesterday. He swore off liquor for good.

Frankie paid his bill, bought gas for the Jenny, and headed to Saplingville.

Chapter Twenty-Six

Al poured Frankie a cup of coffee. "Well, I see you and Miss Priss had fun at the New Year's Eve Party."

Frankie drank a swig and put his cup on the floor. "Yes, we did." He pulled a cigarette from his pocket and placed it on the table with a matchbox. "She played me." He reached for his coffee cup.

Al tilted his head. "Whatcha mean, played you? She acted like she could eat you for breakfast."

He held his cup with both hands. "I mean, she ain't changed. Still the same ol' Ruthie. Must've been practicing for one of her plays."

"What'd she do?" Al straightened in his chair.

Frankie drank a big swig of coffee, letting it burn his throat as it went down. "We'd planned for me to fly her to Atlanta Saturday afternoon. When I got to her house, Mrs. Douglas informed me Ronald drove her to school. She knew he would drive her back, why'd she lie to me?"

Al drank the last drop of coffee in his cup. "I don't get it. I ain't never wrong about these things, and that girl...that girl, she loves you. There's more to this story than what you know. Can you get in touch with her?"

"I don't know how, and I'm not gonna try. If she wants the dandy instead of me, let her have him. She's nothing but trouble anyway." He lit his cigarette and inhaled the smoke into his lungs.

"Yeah, but you love her, don't you? She's the first one you couldn't tame, ain't she?"

Frankie remembered all the times Ruthie had played him for a fool. "This is the last straw. I'm done."

Al saw Victor arrive and gathered their cups. "Never say never, and don't forget you work for her brother. He might be able to shed some light on this if you ask him."

He tapped his cigarette, ashes tumbled to the floor. "Not going to involve Victor, he's got enough to deal with. I'll handle this my way."

****

Frankie and Lisbeth walked toward the Cessna. "Today we're going to practice landings."

Lisbeth jumped up and down. "I wondered when you would teach me how to land."

"Let's fly around about thirty minutes and review what we've done, then work thirty minutes on your landings."

Lisbeth grabbed the clipboard and started the check list. "How did it feel to land with people standing on the wings?"

He had so many fond memories of his time in the flying circus. "Back then, I had more bravery than smarts."

"It's not how Victor tells it. He says you were the best barnstormer ever."

"I enjoyed it, and I had the safety of others to consider. That'll make you nail a three-point landing."

Lisbeth finished the check list, and they settled in their seats.

Frankie observed how she checked the gauges and started the plane like a seasoned professional. "You take off; let's see if you remember what I taught you before Christmas."

The plane headed down the runway and lifted into the air. When they were flying at a safe altitude, she said, "I'm glad you and Ruth Ann got together. I've never seen her so happy."

He didn't want to involve Lisbeth, but he had to know. "Did she mention Ronald? She wanted me to fly her to Atlanta, but when I arrived at your house, Mrs. Douglas said she left with him."

"I wasn't home. I was under the impression you flew her. Ma didn't mention anything to me about Ronald."

Frankie changed the subject. "You're flying real smooth now. Remember when you first started and how you had to struggle to keep the plane steady?"

"Yes, I do. It feels like second nature now."

Lisbeth changed course and headed for the runway.

He instructed her on landing the plane and the first landing the wheels bumped the runway but she kept the plane under control. "Real good for a first try."

Lisbeth made a smooth take-off. She flew around in a circle and headed for the airstrip.

He was impressed with the next landing. "Excellent."

She smiled and shut down the engine. "I'll do my solo flight before you know it."

Ruth Ann and Lisbeth are as different as day and night. How can they be sisters? "Lisbeth, you're the best student I've ever taught. I'm proud of you."

"Thanks Frankie. I'm honored you think so."

****

Frankie sat at his desk making a list of supplies he

needed to repair a customer's plane.

Victor grabbed a chair and sat. "Hey, man. I haven't had a chance to talk to you. Great to see you and Ruth Ann together."

He put his pencil down. "Yeah, well, it didn't last long."

Victor rolled his eyes, stared at the ceiling, and let out a breath. "What'd she do this time?"

Frankie hesitated. "Victor, I don't want to get you involved in this."

Victor crossed his arms and gave him a questioning look. "I'm involved. She's my sister, and wild as she is, I love her. I've never seen her so happy."

He decided he'd better tell Victor the truth...well, most of it. "I arrived at her house Saturday afternoon, and your mother met me on the porch, said Ronald drove her to Atlanta."

"I'm sorry, man. She didn't mention anything to us about him coming to Saplingville. In fact, she didn't mention Ronald at all to me or Dottie. You are going with us to Atlanta to see her play?"

Frankie grabbed his pencil and started writing. "No, I don't think I'll be able to."

"I hope you change your mind. I don't blame you for being angry, but there may be more to the story. We haven't heard her side, yet." Victor stood and placed the chair against the wall.

He kept his temper in check, blood's thicker than water. "If she tells you any different, you can let me know."

Victor headed to his office. "I will."

Chapter Twenty-Seven

Frankie worked long hours and took on a few more students. He stayed busy in an effort to forget about Ruthie. He hated to admit Ronald beat him. He missed her, and he'd never forget how it felt to hold her in his arms and glide across the dance floor. Sometimes he regretted he'd stopped her when she seduced him at the hangar. At least he would know what it felt like to possess her body. He wanted to marry her, make love to her every day of their life. She was the last thing he thought about before he drifted to sleep and the first thing he remembered each morning.

Victor purchased a Stinson Trimotor which held ten passengers. Frankie worked on Sunday afternoons selling rides in the airplane. The first Sunday five people paid for a ride. A man and his son stayed behind asking about the plane, wanting to see the engines and how the plane worked. The father said if he had money, he'd take flying lessons and the son talked about joining the service so he could learn to fly. Frankie wanted to give the man his two dollars back, but the sharecropper, a poor but proud man, wanted a better life for his son, and this once in a lifetime experience would show him there were possibilities beyond their little town.

The next Sunday, he had eighteen people standing in line when he arrived. He took the plane up twice to accommodate everyone. Since then, he had a steady stream of customers and flew the plane at least three times each Sunday. He kept the plane in the air for thirty minutes and let the passengers see their town from the sky.

Frankie arrived at work Monday morning and headed to Victor's office. "Morning, boss. Here's your seventy-five percent from yesterday's plane rides."

Victor studied a map and motioned for him to sit. "How many yesterday?"

He sat in the chair facing his boss. "Twenty-five."

"Man, I figured we'd have two or three each Sunday, never dreamed you'd have to take it up three times." Victor folded the map.

"It's a great ship. I love to fly it." He nodded toward the map. "Planning a trip?"

Victor opened the top drawer of his desk and retrieved a piece of paper. "Here's a list of companies I'm contacting and offering our services. You may be flying the company heads to meetings and such. You interested? I'll pay you extra."

Frankie studied the list. "Sure, the more flying time I have the better I like it."

"You'll have to stay over in a hotel if their meetings go for a few days. I know what a homebody you are." Victor pulled out the telephone directory.

"No problem. I'll handle it." He passed the list back to his boss.

"Thanks. I knew I could count on you. I'm using the plane this weekend to take everyone to Atlanta to see the play." Victor stared. "You comin' with us?"

He struggled to keep his face from showing any emotion but he felt the blood rise to his cheeks. "No, I won't be able to make it. Y'all have fun. Who's going?"

"Everyone except Walter, Delores, Avery and Annie. Delores refuses to fly, and Walter doesn't want to leave her. Avery and Annie are staying at our house with the twins. Ruth Ann will be disappointed if you don't come."

Frankie's lips parted, and he closed them. He couldn't say what he wanted. "Y'all have a good time." He couldn't see her with Ronald, his heart was already broken, he didn't need her to stomp on it, too.

On Friday afternoon, Frankie and Al readied the Stinson Trimotor for the weekend. Frankie checked the mechanical end of the plane, and Al cleaned and polished the interior.

He climbed in the pilot's seat while Al cleaned the windshield on the co-pilot side. "You've got it looking good in here. Victor's family will be mighty impressed."

Al ran his rag over the instruments encased in glass. "I think you should go. Check out what she's been doin'."

Frankie's heart pounded in his chest. "I know what she's been up to. I don't want to see her with the dandy."

Al continued to clean. "You're mad and you've got reason to be but I think there's more to this story than meets the eye. You'll never have any peace until you know."

He jumped to the ground. "Guess I'll never have any peace."

Chapter Twenty-Eight

Ruth Ann stood in the wings and willed her hands to stop shaking. She inhaled a long, slow breath and felt her diaphragm expand. She exhaled all the air from her lungs and started again. She'd be fine once she stepped on the stage. She glanced through the crack in the curtain searching for Frankie. The lights were dim in the theater, and she couldn't see anyone. She stood back stage listening and waiting for her entrance. She said a silent prayer.

The moment her foot hit the stage the fear disappeared, she and the universe were one. Only when Act Four ended and the actors were called on stage for a curtain call did she gaze at the crowd. She spotted her family clapping and waving. Frankie was not with them. The curtain fell, and the actors dispersed to their dressing rooms. She shared a room with five other girls, excitement and energy from the performance permeated the space. She stepped out of her period costume and hung it on a rack with the others. She dressed in her street clothes and shoes and raced out the door.

She hurried to the front of the theater where her family waited.

Hattie grabbed her daughter and hugged her. "You were wonderful. I'm so proud of you."

Jacob put his arm around her shoulder. "Great job."

Victor, Dottie, and Lisbeth took turns hugging and

congratulating her.

She tried not to sound disappointed. "Where's Frankie?"

Her mother narrowed her eyes. "Why would he come to your play?" Contempt filled her voice.

The hatred spilling from her mother's eyes made her step back. "Because he promised."

Ronald approached, and she changed the subject. "So, did y'all like the play?"

Hattie met Ronald with a hug. "Ronald, you were wonderful. I enjoyed seeing you and Ruth Ann act together."

He shook hands with everyone. "I've had a fun time working with Ruth Ann, she's a wonderful actress. Now, if I can convince her to go the New York with me after graduation. I think she should try her hand at stage acting in the big city."

Her mother's face broke into a huge smile. "We can plan a June wedding after you graduate."

His face went white before he returned Mrs. Douglas' smile with one of his own.

Ruth Ann watched as her father sized Ronald, it'd be a cold day in hell before Ronald pulled the wool over her daddy's eyes. She tugged Victor to the side and whispered. "I want to have lunch with y'all tomorrow before you go. Family only, I'm not telling Ronald."

Victor wrote the name of their hotel. "This is where we're staying. Call in the morning, and we'll decide where to meet. I begged Frankie to come, but he's upset about you not telling him about Ronald driving you to school."

She recalled the events of the day. "I gave Ma a

note to give him. I didn't know Ronald was coming to Saplingville." Coldness filled her belly. She stared at the woman who gave birth to her and recognized her for the conniving, cruel person she was. *Of course he was mad, he didn't get the note.*

Victor shook his head. "Frankie didn't mention anything about a note." He regarded his sister. "Ma never gave it to him."

She glared at her mother, laughing and talking to Ronald. "No, she didn't. Frankie will never speak to me again."

Ronald kissed Mrs. Douglas' hand and stepped toward Ruth Ann. "I'll get your girl to her place. Great to see all of you."

She watched as her family made their way to the waiting taxi cabs. Remorse filled the pit of her stomach, and she ignored Ronald's constant babble. They approached her building and she unlocked the door, and Ronald started inside. She put her hand on his chest. "I'm tired. You need to go so I can get some rest."

He pushed his way inside, closed the door, and crushed her into the wall kissing her and toying with the buttons on her dress. She struggled but he had her pinned. She shoved harder, "Ronald, stop. I mean it."

He cupped her breast. "No, you don't. You know you want this as much as I do."

Her emotions hit the breaking point. Tears spilled from her eyes.

He stepped away. "Did I hurt you? I'm sorry if I did. With all the work and rehearsals, I've missed us." He tilted his head and lifted her chin with his hand, "I miss you."

Tears streamed down her face. "Go, please."

He pulled a handkerchief from his pocket and placed it in her hand. "Get some rest. I'll see you tomorrow. I know how emotional it is to be in your first play."

She closed the door and stumbled to the settee. Her mother wanted her to be with Ronald, but she couldn't believe she would do such a thing. As Ruth Ann got older, she saw a side of Hattie she didn't like. Her mother hurt Frankie yet regarded Ronald as an angel...if she knew the truth. Guilt poured over her. Her mother was right about one thing. She had two boys vying for her affection. She had to decide. It didn't matter what choice she made. Frankie would never forgive her for this.

The next day, she took a trolley to the restaurant to meet her family for lunch. She entered the café and approached the round table.

Victor stood and helped her into her chair. "Glad you could join us before we go home."

She sat as Victor adjusted her chair. "This is a treat for me. I don't leave campus often."

Lisbeth put her menu on the table. "When are you coming home again?"

"In a couple of weeks." She turned toward her brother. "Victor can you fly me home two weeks from today?"

He looked up from his menu. "I'd be happy to."

She faced her sister. "How are the flying lessons?"

Lisbeth gave Ruth Ann her full attention. "Great. I've learned to land and take-off. Frankie's the best teacher."

Victor interrupted, "Frankie says you're the best student he's ever had."

Hattie glared at her daughter and spat her words, "Where's Ronald?"

She refused eye contact with her mother and stared at her menu, "I wanted to be with my family. Ronald and I aren't joined at the hip."

Jacob patted his wife's hand. "Ruth Ann, don't you have another performance today?"

"Yes. I have one tonight and another tomorrow afternoon."

Jacob stared at his daughter, their eyes met in understanding. "I wanted to tell you again how well you did and how proud I am. I can't imagine how much work it takes to memorize the lines and become the part of the person you play on stage. I'm sorry I didn't encourage you more."

Her eyes filled with tears. She appreciated his compliment, and the look in his eye assured her he was on her side, not her mother's. "Thanks, Pa."

After lunch, they gathered on the sidewalk. She pulled her mother aside. "Ma, did you give the note to Frankie like I asked you?" She watched her mother; she had to know the truth.

Hattie's face flushed red. "What note? Did you give me a note?"

"You know I did. It had Frankie's name on it. You were supposed to give it to him when he arrived."

Hattie took a deep breath and licked her lips. She put her hand on Ruth Ann's arm. "No, I didn't. He's no good for you. Ronald can give you so much more than Frankie can.

Ruth Ann turned away. She didn't want to argue in front of everyone.

Her mother jerked her around to face her. She

glanced at her husband and lowered her voice. "When did Frankie become so special anyway? You never liked him. After Frankie got married and Audrey left him, you chased after him like a bitch in heat. I don't understand you."

The words her mother spoke cut her like a razor blade. She no longer cared who heard them, her voice rose to almost a shout. "That's right Ma, you've never understood me. Whoever I decide to spend my life with is my choice, not yours."

She marched to the trolley stop and didn't take a backward glance.

Chapter Twenty-Nine

Frankie had his head in the engine of the Stinson Trimotor performing the routine maintenance when Victor arrived at the hangar Monday morning. He grabbed a rag and stepped off the small step ladder. "Did ya have a good trip?"

Victor walked toward the airplane. "Dottie and I enjoyed ourselves, but we were glad to get home and see the babies."

"Careful, Victor, the stork may make another visit to your house." Frankie gave him a knowing smile.

"Man, if he does, it was worth it. Haven't had Dottie to myself in a long time."

He worked to remove the grease from his hands. "How was the play?"

"You mean how was Ruth Ann?"

His stomach filled with emptiness and dread. Did he really want to know? He hesitated, "Yeah, her too."

"She's a very good actress. I had to remind myself she was my sister. She asked about you." Victor stared and waited for him to respond.

"Did she now?" He searched through the tools for a screw driver.

"She's coming home in two weeks."

"The dandy coming with her?" Frankie walked toward the plane anxious to end the conversation.

"No, I think she's trying to cool it. Did you have

many customers yesterday?"

"I had twenty-nine. I left the money in your desk drawer. We'll have this airplane paid off before you know it." He climbed the stepladder and continued his work.

Victor checked the box for mail and headed inside the hangar. "I hope so. I didn't think we would do this well selling airplane rides."

He loved being right. "I've told you for years people want to fly."

Victor responded. "I should have listened to you before now."

He continued his work. *So, Ruthie cooled it off with Ronald which meant, she never stopped seeing him.* He felt like someone twisted a knife in his gut.

Chapter Thirty

Ruth Ann arrived at the Theatre Arts Building early and headed to her methods class. She rounded the corner hall and saw two people kissing. As she got closer, she recognized Ronald and Jenny Price. She stopped and observed familiar moves. *How many of the girls in the class was he seeing?* She tiptoed around them and slipped to her classroom. A few minutes later he and Jenny wandered into the room. She leered at him.

He eased to her desk. "It's not what you think."

The walls closed in around her. She had to get away. Jenny stared at her with a smug smile. She took her books and left the classroom.

Ronald bolted out of the room explaining his actions.

She ignored him. She retrieved her key from her bag. Her hand shook and she couldn't get it in the lock.

He snatched the key and opened the door. "We need to talk."

She put her books on the table beside the door. "Come in, let's talk."

He sat on the settee and motioned her to sit. Instead, she sat in the chair waiting for him to say something.

He broke the silence. "Ruth Ann, you send me mixed signals. One minute we're necking and I feel like you want me, and the next minute you're avoiding me. I told you I loved you, but you don't say it to me."

A tear ran down her face. "You don't tell a girl you love them and then kiss another girl. Is it because I won't go all the way with you?"

"I want you. I've never denied it. We're adults now. We don't have to get married to have intimacy."

For the first time, she recognized Ronald for what he was. "So, all this talk about going to New York together. You want me to come with you and live with you for the nooky. What if I got knocked up? You'd dump me and find someone else." Her cheeks heated in anger.

He reached for her hands, she pulled them away. "Neither of us have worked this hard to become actors to get married and live the lives of our parents. I know you don't want that any more than I do." He tilted his head and placed his hand on her arm.

She jerked away and glared at this man she thought she knew. "No, you're right. I will have a career as an actress or a teacher, but I will live a decent, honest life. What you're asking me to do is against everything my parents taught me."

He scooped her from her chair and kissed her. "I'm sorry. I know I did wrong. Let's see where the road takes us."

She couldn't blame Ronald. She'd treated Frankie the same way. She was no better than him. "Yes, we'll see how things go. We have several more weeks before graduation, and both of us have decisions to make."

He made his way to class. She closed the door, settled in a chair, and gathered her thoughts before she returned to class. Ronald confused her. She didn't think she cared about him until she saw him kissing Jenny. She had to see Frankie and sort out her feelings. If, he would talk to her after what her mother did. After what she did.

Chapter Thirty-One

Frankie maneuvered tables and tool boxes out of the way so Al could sweep and mop the floor of the hangar.

The janitor bent to gather pieces of paper. "You don't have to help me. I can handle this stuff."

Al could do it, but he wanted to help the old man. "I know you can, but four hands make easy work. You help me with propping the planes and other things when I need an extra hand."

He watched Victor as he hung up the phone in the office and head toward them. "Frankie, I need for you to do me a favor. Ruth Ann needs a flight home, but Dottie called and she has something for us to do tomorrow. Are you available?"

He shuffled a couple of chairs. He didn't want to see Ruthie, much less fly her home. He hesitated hoping Victor would see he didn't want to go and take back the request. When the air was heavy and Al gave him a questioning glance, he responded, "Sure thing, boss."

Victor walked to the door and turned. "Great, I told her to be at the airport at noon. Thanks for doing this for us. I'm headed home; see y'all later."

Al leaned his broom against a wall. "Are you going to be good with this, son?"

He stared at his desk and remembered how Ruthie

tempted him in the very place he stood. "It's a job, nothing more. I fly air taxis all the time."

Al studied Frankie's face. "Be careful and concentrate on your flying. You'll have too much time alone with her in the plane, and I don't want you two arguing like a couple of cats in heat."

The solution formed in his brain. "Won't be any alone time. I'm taking the Jenny tomorrow. I wouldn't be able to hear her talk if I wanted to."

Al shook his head. "For the love of Pete, don't take that plane. You don't fly her much anymore, the other planes are safer and you'll get to Atlanta and back faster."

"You're right about one thing. The Jenny needs flying. Let's go check her out and get her ready for tomorrow."

Al continued the argument, "Who'll prop you off? We won't be here to help you."

"Mr. Andrews will do it for me." He gathered some tools and the oil can. "Here, take these, and I'll get the gas can. Let's go."

Al threw the tools and some rags into a small toolbox. "You are one stubborn jackass."

****

Frankie arrived at Candler Field early. He stood by the JN-Four watching for Ruthie's taxi. A crowd gathered around his biplane. Four pretty women and three men asked questions. He helped the women onto the wing one by one so they could look inside.

Ruthie's taxi arrived, and she walked toward the plane. She stood off to the side watching.

Frankie ignored her. He gave each girl a hug and shook hands with the men. "My client's here, got to get going. Glad you liked the plane, and if you are in Saplingville, stop by Andrews Field, and I'll give you a free ride."

The group fell away, and Ruthie shuffled closer. "So you're my ride home." He didn't look at her, just reached for her suitcase.

He placed her bag in the front seat and handed her the aviator cap and goggles. "Yep, I'm your taxi service for today."

She struggled with her hat, stuffing her thick hair under it. "Frankie, I've got to talk to you about something. I gave Ma a note for you before I left. I didn't know…"

He interrupted, "I didn't get a note. Now climb in the airplane and let's go." He searched the hangar for someone to prop them off.

Frankie and the attendant guided the Jenny to the runway. He jumped in, and the man propped the plane. The Jenny lifted into the air. He relaxed in his seat and stared at the back of Ruthie's head. He'd never known a woman who could make him love her one minute and hate her, the next. Mrs. Douglas would have given him the note. She invented the excuse, he didn't buy it. He thanked God for this warm spring day so he could fly the Jenny. He didn't want to make conversation or argue. As soon as they landed, he'd take her home.

He settled in his seat and enjoyed the blue sky. The sound of the engine changed; he detected a slight sputter. He replaced the spark plugs a month ago, and he and Al greased the valve gear yesterday. He would give her a good overhaul next week.

When flying a plane like the JN-Four, a pilot always keeps his eye open for a place to land. Frankie made several unexpected landings both as a barnstormer and in his recreational flying. He didn't want to do it with Ruthie in the plane and prayed they would make it to the farm.

He straightened in his seat and listened for any indication of trouble. He gazed down and relaxed, open fields as far as he could see. The miles passed, they neared home as the fields changed into timberland. With no warning of trouble, the engine coughed, RPM dropped, the engine caught, sped up, then coughed and sputtered and became quiet. He checked the magnetos, carb heat, and throttle control. Nothing changed. The engine was dead. Slowly windmilling, he trimmed the airplane for best glide speed, and the prop windmilled without a sound. *Probably a broken fuel line. Now, where to land?* He straightened in his seat and searched for a place.

Nothing but treetops. His heart raced, his face wet with perspiration. *Don't panic.* He peered ahead and watched Ruthie's head tilt. He figured she was either praying or scared out of her mind. He searched to the right, thank God, a field. He guided the plane toward it, checking wind direction by the drift of the plane and smoke coming from the chimney of a nearby house. He studied the ground and made a quick assessment as to how much room he had to land. The field appeared clear except for a huge oak tree with cows grazing beneath. He had to stop the Jenny before it hit the tree. He side-slipped the plane down, then straightened out for a firm landing, and stopped short of the tree. The plane hit the ground hard but stayed in one piece. Cows scattered, running in all directions. He unfastened his seatbelt and jumped on the wing.

Ruthie's head hit the front of the plane when they landed, and he wanted to make sure she was all right. Her body folded over the seatbelt. He wrestled her upright to unfasten the belt. Blood oozed from a gash on her head. She didn't respond when he called her name. He peered around the pasture to make sure no bulls lurked. Several cows and a donkey but no bull, so he removed her from the plane and leaned her against the tree. He felt her pulse; she was alive. He pulled out his pocket knife and cut enough fabric from the bottom of his t-shirt to tie around her head. Blood oozed through the material. He put pressure on the wound until the bleeding stopped then cut more fabric and tied it around her head.

He sat and gathered her into his lap. He closed his eyes and willed his body to stop shaking. He rocked her in his arms and prayed. "Dear Jesus, please let her be okay. Ruthie, I'm so sorry." A tear rolled down his face into the stubble of his beard. He feared his heart would beat out of his chest. His gaze wandered to the Jenny, and he realized how lucky they were to find a place to land. "Dear God, please, I love her so much, don't take her from me."

Ruth Ann squirmed and snuggled her head against his shoulder.

"Ruthie, wake up." He tilted her head. "Open your eyes."

She grabbed his arm for support. She focused her eyes on him, then the airplane.

He gazed toward heaven. "Thank you," he whispered.

She struggled to sit. "What happened?"

"The engine stopped, we had to land in this field.

You have a bad cut on your forehead."

She put her hand on the bandage tied around her head. "My head hurts."

He put his hand on her chin and examined her face. He wanted to kiss her fear and cuts and bruises away, but too much had changed since the last time they were together.

She put her arms around his neck. "Frankie, I'm so sorry about what happened with Ma and the note and Ronald and everything I've ever done or said to hurt you."

He put his index finger on her mouth. "Don't talk, precious. Rest, I'll get us out of this. I'm going to have to leave you here and get help."

She grabbed his arm. "What about the cows?"

"They won't hurt you. I'll be as quick as I can." He heard the horse hooves approaching and jumped to his feet. A man on horseback rode toward them.

The man jumped off his horse and ran. "I saw the plane come down. Are y'all hurt?"

Frankie gazed toward the sky and thanked God for sparing their lives and sending someone to help. He shook the man's hand. "Ruthie hit her head and needs a doctor, but I'm fine. I'm Frankie Howard, sorry about landing in your field."

"Harvey Johnson, and I'm glad you're okay. Where were you heading?"

"Andrews Field."

"You're about fifteen miles from Saplingville, I can take you in my car. When I return, I'll put the cows in another pasture so they won't bother your plane." He and Frankie lifted Ruthie and steadied her.

He put his arm around her waist. "Thanks, the

cows like to lick the wings of the plane; they're attracted to the glue. I'll return as soon as I can and fix it."

Mr. Johnson checked her forehead and surveyed her eyes. "You may have a concussion, young lady. We need to get you to a doctor. We'll put you on the horse, and I'll ride you to the house. Frankie, you're on your own."

"No problem, Mr. Johnson. Do you have a phone?"

"Yes, anyone I can call?"

Frankie nodded to Ruthie. "Yes, call her parents, Mr. and Mrs. Jacob Douglas, Saplingville and tell them what happened. Ask if they can get the doctor to see her when we arrive."

He followed the horse and struggled to keep up. His right ankle hurt, and his neck ached. He rolled his head around trying to loosen his muscles. The landing was hard, but at least they weren't killed and the JN-Four stood in one piece. The Jenny wasn't the most reliable plane, but if he had to be in an emergency, he'd rather be in the Jenny, it glided easier than other planes. Frankie wanted to run, he longed to be with Ruthie, but his ankle wouldn't let him. Mr. Johnson kept the horse in his eye sight so he wouldn't get lost. He spotted the stand of pines he had flown over and the horse stop. The man pointed in the direction they were headed. He made his way through the trees and joined them at the white, two-story house set back from the road, nestled under the pines.

Mr. Johnson had his truck facing down the drive, and Ruthie sat in the front seat. He climbed in, "Did you get in touch with her parents?"

He put the truck in gear. "I talked to Mr. Douglas.

He said he would have the doctor at the house when we arrive."

Ruthie placed her head on Frankie's shoulder, and he cradled her hands in his. Her skin felt cold and clammy. "Don't go to sleep, you may have a concussion."

She sighed. "But I'm so sleepy. Let me sleep 'til we get home."

Mr. Johnson nodded to Frankie. "No, he's right don't go to sleep until you see the doctor. I'll have you home as fast as I can."

Chapter Thirty-Two

Frankie gave Mr. Johnson directions to the Douglas house and cradled Ruthie with his left arm, kissing the top of her head and thanking God they survived. He relived the emergency landing wondering how the journey fell apart, what he could have done to prevent it. The truck pulled in the gravel drive.

Hattie paced on the front porch. When the truck entered the drive, she ran down the steps. "Is she all right?"

Frankie scooped Ruthie in his arms and raced toward the house. "Yes, I think so." He held her close, her arms clinched around his neck.

Hattie followed. "The doctor's waiting in the parlor."

He placed her on the sofa. His heart pounded in his eardrum. He looked around the quiet room and wondered if the others heard it.

Dr. Herschel grabbed his bag. "Everyone out, except Mrs. Douglas."

He stared at his girl and backed to the door. The room spun, and he grabbed the door frame for support.

Mr. Douglas put his hand on his arm to steady him. "Let's go to the kitchen, son."

He stumbled to the kitchen with Mr. Douglas and Mr. Johnson on each side holding him up.

They pulled a chair out for him. He plopped down

and rested his head in his hands.

Mr. Douglas sat and put his hand on Frankie's arm. "You all right?"

He raised his head. "I will be when I find out she is."

"You two walking away from the emergency landing and making it home is a miracle in itself. Everything's going to be fine." He placed glasses, plates, and forks on the table and lifted the lid off the metal cake saver. "Both of you need something to eat and drink." He poured sweet tea and cut pieces of pound cake. "Thanks, Mr. Johnson, for your kindness in driving Frankie and my daughter home. I'd like to give you some money for gas and your time."

Mr. Johnson drank tea and ate the cake. "Not necessary, I'm glad they're safe. I saw the plane coming down. I don't know how Frankie kept it out of the trees, but it glided straight for the pasture. I saddled the horse and raced to them, it amazed me the plane was in one piece and they were alive."

Mr. Douglas smiled and nodded toward the pilot. "If anyone could land a plane and avoid a crash, it would be Frankie. You know he was one of the best barnstormers in the country."

Frankie sipped his tea and stared at the cake. *Famous barnstormer, hell, famous idiot's more like it.* "I really messed up this time."

Mr. Douglas placed his hand on Frankie's shoulder. "It's not your fault. You're a hero. Your actions saved my little girl's life."

He ran his fingers through the condensation on the tea glass. "I should have taken another plane. The Jenny's getting old, and she's not as reliable as she used to be."

Mr. Douglas regarded the fly boy. "Could you land another plane without incident?"

He considered the question, if this happened in another plane, they'd be dead. "Probably not."

"Well now. We have our answer. Everything's going to be fine."

Frankie wrote Mr. Johnson's address and phone number on a piece of paper. "Is Monday morning soon enough to get my plane from your property?"

Mr. Johnson said, "No problem, and I'll put the cows in another enclosure as soon as I get home."

Dr. Herschel entered the kitchen. "Ruth Ann's fine. Hattie and I got her to her bedroom, she's resting. She has a slight concussion, and the cut on her forehead required a couple of stitches. She needs bed rest for a week, and then she should be able to resume regular activities. I'll come by Monday."

Mr. Johnson stood and shook hands with Frankie and Mr. Douglas. "I'll be going. See you Monday, Frankie."

Frankie sat in his chair. He didn't want to face Mrs. Douglas, but he had to.

Mr. Douglas walked to the kitchen door. "I'm going to check on her, want to come?"

He didn't budge from his chair. "No, I'm going to sit here for a few minutes. I do want to see her before I leave."

When Jacob entered her room, Hattie headed downstairs. "Is Frankie still here?"

Jacob sat by the bed and stroked his daughter's face checking for a fever. "He's in the kitchen."

Ruth Ann raised her voice. "Ma, don't be hard on

him, he did the best he could."

She entered the kitchen. Frankie stood. "Mrs. Douglas, I'm so sorry. It's all my fault. I wouldn't hurt Ruthie for anything."

She put her arms around Frankie's neck and started crying. "I'm so glad you're not hurt. You saved my daughter's life. Thank God you're both alive."

He expected the woman to bless him out; he deserved it. But her tears and her sincere concern for his life surprised him. A tear slipped down his face. "I'm so sorry."

She stepped back and looked up at him. "No, Frankie, I'm sorry."

"About what?" He watched as she busied herself in the kitchen.

She opened the refrigerator and poured some cold water in a glass for her daughter. "Frankie, you're like a son to me, and I've wronged you. I knew you were going to fly her to school, but when Ronald arrived, I made her go. She gave me a note for you, and I burned it."

He stumbled to his chair. "Why?"

"I thought Ronald would be a better match. I promise to stay out of your business. I made mistakes at her age, and I didn't want her to follow in my footsteps. I know now she has to make up her own mind. Do you forgive me?"

He sat in the chair and digested the information. Ruthie had told him the truth. He reached for the glass of cold water. "Yes, ma'am, I forgive you. Can I take her this?"

She nodded and dried her face with the hem of her apron. "Of course."

He took the steps two at a time, blocking out the pain in his ankle.

Mr. Douglas saw him at the door and stood. "Here, Frankie, sit a while. I'm going downstairs."

He lifted Ruthie and gave her the glass of water. She sipped a small amount. "Drink a little more," he urged.

She grasped the glass with both hands and drank. "Thanks for taking care of me."

He put the glass on the night stand and tucked her in bed. "I didn't do such a good job. You could have been killed."

She grabbed his hand. "You could have, too, but we weren't. When the propeller stopped turning and the engine died, I was scared to death, but you took care of us."

Tears dripped from his eyes, he swiped them with his hand. "If anything had happened to you... I can't stand to think about it."

She swung her legs to the side of the bed to sit closer. "Frankie, I'm here; you're here. We're safe."

He scooped her from the bed and cradled her in his arms. "I love you. You are the most precious thing in my life."

She cradled his face in her hands. "I love you, Frankie Howard. I'm so sorry about everything. Will you ever forgive me?"

He held her in his arms until his ankle wouldn't take it. He gave her a gentle kiss, then lost himself in the moment making up for their time apart. He placed her in the bed and tucked the quilt around her. "I'll forgive you if you'll forgive me for thinking the worst. Victor and Al tried to reason with me, but I was a stubborn jackass."

She grabbed his hand and kissed it, giving him a wink. "You're my stubborn jackass."

He stood over her wishing he could crawl in bed with her. "I'll see you tomorrow. You need to rest."

He limped the few blocks to his house. He planned to soak his ankle and take some aspirin for his neck.

He sat in his front room reading a book when he heard a knock. He grabbed his crutch and hobbled to the door.

Just as he expected. "Victor, I wondered how long it would take for you to hear about the emergency landing."

Victor stepped in the house and stared at his friend. "I didn't know you were hurt. Did Dr. Herschel check you out?"

He limped to the sofa. "No, to tell you the truth, I didn't think about it. My concern was Ruthie. I twisted my ankle, and my neck's sore. I'm soaking the ankle, using crutches, and taking aspirin. Not much else I can do. Have you seen her?"

Victor sat in the chair. "I saw her before going to the newspaper office. They called as soon as they heard about the incident and wanted a statement. She doesn't remember anything after the engine stopped. I think she fainted."

Frankie ran his hand through his hair. "Makes sense. I saw her head drop, and she slumped in her seat, I figured she knelt her head in prayer or was just scared as hell. It's why she hit her head, she didn't brace for the landing."

Victor said, "Well, you're the hero of the day. The Saplingville newspaper interviewed me. You'll be in the papers tomorrow. I told them if not for your experience as a barnstormer, this would have been a disaster. I even gave them a picture of you and me standing in front of the Jenny. You might make the front page."

He adjusted his foot on the coffee table. "It didn't take them long to jump on this story. I don't feel like a hero. I feel like an idiot to let this happen. I hope this doesn't cause a problem with the business."

Victor replied with excitement in his voice. "Are you kidding? Everyone will want to fly with you now. What happened? Did you have any warning?"

"I heard a few sputters and coughs and lost power. I didn't get a chance to check, but I figure a fuel line problem. We flew over a stand of pines and God opened them and a pasture appeared. I had to side-slip in to get down in the distance I had and make a firm landing. Ruthie fell forward. The blow caused a deep slash to her forehead, and she bled like a stuck pig. I pulled her from the plane. She stayed out for a few minutes. The longest minutes of my life, I'll tell ya."

Victor studied his friend. "But she isn't dead, neither are you. Your skill and quick thinking saved you both. Stop beating yourself over it."

Frankie inhaled a deep breath and exhaled, the picture of Ruthie's bloody head never left his mind. "You're right, as usual. I've experienced worse situations but never with anyone in the plane. It's different when you're responsible for another person."

Victor uncrossed his leg and moved to the edge of his chair. "Yeah, what if you had a wife and twins."

He imagined Ruthie and him with a child, a boy, no, a girl that looked just like her. "I wish I did."

Victor stood to go. "Can I get you anything?"

Frankie grabbed his crutch and stood. "No, I'm good for now. Can you stop by for me Monday morning? My car's at the airfield, and I won't need it tomorrow. I advised Mr. Johnson we'd get the Jenny fixed and out of his pasture Monday."

Victor stopped at the door and turned. "We'll take all the tools and another fuel line. See you Monday morning." He put his hand on Frankie's shoulder. "Remember, all landings you can walk away from are good landings."

"You got that right." He gave Victor a pat on the back. "Thanks, man, for everything."

****

Frankie woke Sunday morning burning with the desire to see Ruthie. He had trouble sleeping because every time he closed his eyes the memory of the Jenny hitting the pasture caused his body to jump. He dozed off around three and slept until ten. The swelling in his ankle had reduced, but his neck hurt worse. He tugged on his no collar gray V-neck shirt and his denim pants. He left the top buttons of his shirt open. He didn't feel like dressing fancy and planned to spend the day with his girl.

He hobbled without his crutches to get his paper. His ankle didn't cooperate, and as bad as he hated, he would have to use his crutch today.

The story made the front page. Frankie laughed when he saw the photograph of him and Victor beside the Jenny. The picture they used was from four years ago when Victor arrived home from the Army Air Corps. The two of them smiling beside the JN-Four. Victor loved the plane as much as he did, and they spent every spare minute they had flying.

Frankie read the story.

LOCAL MAN SAVES THE DAY

Frankie Howard, former barnstormer now working as a mechanic, air taxi driver, and flight instructor was on a routine air taxi run to Candler Field in Atlanta. On his return to Saplingville, he had to make an emergency landing in a pasture. Mr. Howard's employer, Victor Douglas, owner of Andrews Field said Mr. Howard's vast experience and knowledge of flying prevented a disaster. The passenger is resting at home with minor injuries. Mr. Douglas said the cause was mechanical failure. The Curtiss JN-Four Biplane was built in 1918. Mr. Douglas has several newer planes used for air taxis, but the Jenny, as they lovingly refer to the JN-Four is Mr. Howard's favorite airplane to fly. Mr. Howard used this very plane for his barnstorming tricks. Frankie Howard joined a barnstorming team in 1924 as a gofer and rose to head pilot in 1927 at the age of 18. The team disbanded in 1932, and Mr. Howard bought the JN-Four and returned to Saplingville. Most Sundays, you can find Mr. Howard at Andrews Field taking people for rides in a Stinson Trimotor.

He put the paper on the coffee table and smiled. No mention of Ruthie. The article would scare people away or spark their curiosity. He hoped for the latter.

Chapter Thirty-Three

Frankie put his flat cap on his head and grabbed his crutch. He'd waited until the Douglas' were done with lunch before going. He didn't want to cause more trouble. He trekked the few blocks using his crutch to keep the weight off his hurt ankle. He'd analyzed all the what ifs since the landing. Today his mind wandered to what he should have done, like he should have taken another plane. He had to see Ruthie and make sure she was well. Only that would stop the voices in his head. He hobbled up the front steps and knocked.

Hattie opened the door and motioned him in. "I didn't know you were hurt, too."

He sat in the nearest chair. "No, ma'am, I twisted my ankle, and my neck's sore. I'm not bad hurt. I'll be fine."

She yelled for her husband. "Jacob, please come in here and see about Frankie. He got hurt yesterday but didn't tell us."

Jacob knelt at Frankie's feet. "Take off your shoe so I can examine your foot."

He untied the laces on his two tone oxfords and took off his red argyle sock.

Jacob examined his ankle pressing with his thumb to determine swelling. "Does this hurt?"

He winced from the pain but kept his foot still. "It's sore, but I've had worse when I sprained it as a kid."

Jacob carefully rotated his foot to determine range of motion. "I don't think the ankle is sprained, just a little swollen. What have you done for it?"

"I soaked in warm Epsom salt water and kept my foot elevated. Luckily, I had some crutches. I'm taking aspirin and applying liniment to my foot and ankle."

Jacob stood. "You did the right thing. But you should have called and I would have driven you. I will be taking you home."

He tugged his sock over the tender flesh.

Jacob said, "Leave the shoe off. I'm sure you want to sit with Ruth Ann. We'll put a foot rest next to your chair so you can keep it elevated."

Hattie headed for the kitchen. "Come in here and let me fix you some lunch."

"No, ma'am, I ate at home."

She rebounded, "Well, I'm feeding you supper then."

Ruth Ann stood at the top of the stairs. "Is Frankie here? What's going on?"

Her mother hurried to her room. "Get in bed. He's here, you'll see him. You know what the doctor advised, bed rest for a week."

She put both hands on her head and smoothed her hair. "Tell him to wait five minutes."

She crawled in bed. "Ma, hand me my mirror and comb, please."

Hattie gave her the mirror. "I'll comb your hair."

She gazed in the mirror as her mother fixed her hair. "Looks fine, thanks."

Hattie smoothed her bangs over the bandage on her forehead. "You're still pretty."

Jacob positioned the foot rest beside the chair. "This is for Frankie."

She sat straighter. "Why does he need a foot rest?"

Her pa said, "Frankie twisted his ankle."

"I didn't know he got hurt. How bad?"

Jacob assured her, "Not bad, but he needs to elevate the foot and keep pressure off the ankle. It'll be sore for a few days."

Frankie put a big smile on his face and entered Ruthie's bedroom. "Hey, fly girl, feeling better today?"

She raked her gaze up Frankie's tall frame. "Fly girl? It scared me so bad I fainted. Victor and Lisbeth got the guts in this family. I'm a wimp."

He left his crutch by the door and settled in the chair adjusting the foot rest to accommodate his long legs. "I don't think you're a wimp. None of us would have the nerve to act on stage."

"Yeah, about that. I hoped you would come to my play. You promised you would."

"Yes, and you promised to let me fly you to school. You're the one who left with the dandy."

"You mean Ronald, why do you call him a dandy?"

Frankie's laughter filled the room. "Victor and I gave him the nickname. He smells like Pond's Cream."

She tilted her head. "How do you know what Pond's Extract Vanishing Cream smells like?"

"I was married, remember?"

"How could I forget," she said with contempt in her voice and a frown on her face.

He tilted his head; he'd get the truth out of her. "What did you see in him anyway?"

"Well, for one thing I met him when everyone

thought you were married. And you, you couldn't wait for me until I got out of school?" She crossed her arms.

He scooted to the edge of his chair. "Wait for you, are you kidding? You never gave me the time of day until I met someone else."

"About her, what did you see in her? Oh, never mind, I know. Tight clothes, low cut blouses, big bubs, and blonde hair."

Frankie lowered his voice. "I'm trying my best to forget this chapter in my life, can you?"

She nodded. "Yes, let's never talk about it again."

"Agreed. Now, tell me about Ronald,. Is he still your boyfriend?"

She adjusted her cover. "You get to the point, don't you?"

"Where you're involved I do. If you're still with the dandy, I'm moving on. I'm too old to play games."

"Yes, I mean…it's complicated."

Now we're getting somewhere. Frankie crossed his arms hoping for the whole story. "I'm listening."

She continued, "Ronald started out as a friend. Everyone likes him because he's a good actor, and he lets everyone know he wants to act on stage in New York, and he is good. He asked me to be his girlfriend. You were married, so I decided I should find someone, too." She watched his face for a reaction. "Anyway, it was all right at first and I liked the attention but after you and I got together, I realized he wasn't the one for me. He didn't make me feel like you did. I didn't crave him when he was gone like I did you."

Frankie tried not to smile. "So, what happened when you returned to school after Christmas?"

"We had a play to perform, and I didn't have time

to do anything but study, memorize and rehearse. I avoided him, best I could."

"But you didn't break up with him? He thought you were his girl?" Frankie's face burned red.

"He kept asking me to go to New York with him after graduation. He said we could have a career on stage."

"Did he ask you to marry him?"

She bit her lower lip weighing her answer. "No, he wanted us to live together." She straightened in bed and talked faster. "I caught him kissing another girl and realized what kind of man he is."

Frankie squelched his temper and kept his voice calm. "What kind of man is he?"

"He wanted intimacy, but he didn't want to marry me."

Frankie stood, fists clenched. "That son of a bitch, I'll kill him."

She jumped out of bed and put her arms around his neck. She stood on her tiptoes and kissed his cheek and whispered, "You asked and I told you, if I can get over you marrying the gold digger bitch, you can get over Ronald."

He gathered her in his arms and gave her a deep kiss. Their tongues met, and he drove his into her mouth. He put his hand on her breast and groaned. He could feel her hard nipple through her nightgown. Suddenly he remembered Mrs. Douglas. If she walked in and caught them, he'd be banned from the house. "Get in bed, I'll cover you."

She crawled in bed and adjusted her pillows. "Will you ever forgive me?"

He tucked the cover around her. "You left without

a word, except for the note your mother burned. I was furious when I heard you left with Ronald. Victor and Al wanted me to get in touch with you, but my stubbornness got in the way." He sat in his chair and adjusted the foot rest. "I even flew to Atlanta, sat in the restaurant, had lunch, and flew back home. I broke my promise to you about coming to see your play because as far as I was concerned you chose the dandy over me." He paused, emotion welled in his throat causing his voice to go soft. "God might be trying to tell us something. He opened the pine thicket, so I would find a pasture where we could land. He spared our lives for a reason." He stared into her eyes, losing himself in his want of her. "I don't think we should argue anymore."

She nodded. "Arguing's our way of communicating. I'll tell you a secret. I used to fuss and complain when Victor insisted on you going places with us, but I was disappointed when you didn't go."

He pulled her hand to his mouth, kissed it, and gave her a mischievous smile. "You were a bearcat, but an adorable one. We wasted a lot of time arguing. In the future, no fussin', just lovin'."

She tugged his earlobe. "Deal."

Lisbeth drifted up the stairs and stopped at Ruth Ann's door. "Can I come in?"

Frankie stood to give Lisbeth the chair.

She noticed his shoeless foot and the foot rest. "No worries, I'll sit on the bed. What happened, did you get hurt, too?"

He sat in the chair and put his foot on the stool. "Twisted my ankle. I'm trying to rest today so I can go to work tomorrow. We've got to get the Jenny home."

Lisbeth couldn't contain her excitement. "I'm glad

you're both okay, but was it exciting? I mean the engine dying and landing the plane in the pasture?"

Ruth Ann pushed the covers back and jumped out of bed. "Exciting. Are you insane? The last thing I remember is the eerie quietness after the engine stopped. You know how I hate take offs and landings. Well this added another thing for me to worry about."

He'd have to stop the argument, or the sisters would go on all day. "The JN-Four is easy to glide to a landing, but you need a good flat surface. I wasn't afraid when the engine stopped, but I worried I wouldn't find a spot in time. When I fly the Jenny, I'm always thinking about a place to land but we were over a pine thicket and I didn't see the pasture until the last minute. We were very lucky."

Lisbeth asked, "Can you fix the Jenny so I can fly it and do tricks like you?"

Ruth Ann put her hand over her heart. "Please don't Lisbeth, I'll worry myself to death."

He guided her to the bed and tucked her in. "Calm down, both of you. Yes, Lisbeth, I said I'd teach you how to fly the Jenny, and I will but no, no aerobatics until you have more experience."

She eased against the pillow. "You pilots are a strange lot."

Lisbeth laughed. "Exactly how we feel about you actors."

Hattie entered the room with two plates. "Lisbeth, come eat with us."

Ruth Ann straightened, and Lisbeth placed the pillows behind her. "Thanks, Ma, looks delicious."

"Thank you, your food is the best." Frankie reached for the plate. He finished his supper and said goodbye to everyone.

Jacob followed him to the door. "Let me get my car keys. I'm taking you home. I know you won't take off sick tomorrow, although I wish you would rest one more day."

He put his shoe on and tied the laces. "Victor and I have to get the Jenny home. We've got a lot of work to do in the morning. It's kind of you to take me home."

Chapter Thirty-Four

Frankie, Victor, and Al arrived at Mr. Johnson's farm before eight Monday morning.

Mr. Johnson greeted them. "Need help with anything?"

After Frankie made introductions, he said, "No, we've got it covered. Thank you, though."

Mr. Johnson rambled toward his house. "Let me know if you need me."

Frankie and Victor proceeded ahead of Al. When Frankie saw the light blue biplane with red, white, and blue stripes on the tail, he broke into a run. He wanted to examine the plane closer and make sure of no damage. For many years, the Jenny was all he had.

Victor caught up. "Slow down, we aren't going to a fire. She's not going anywhere."

They walked around the plane checking for damage. Frankie ran his hand over the fabric of the plane. "I don't see any problems on the outside."

They concentrated their attention on the engine. Victor said, "Let's turn her around in the direction you'll take off."

They guided the plane around and heard a loud commotion. Al wrestled the large wagon loaded with tools through the rough grass.

He waved. "The rabbit might win the race, but don't forget the turtle has the tools."

Victor acknowledged the old man. "Thanks, Al. I don't know what we'd do without you." They stepped toward him.

Frankie grabbed the wagon handle and headed toward the Jenny.

Al yelled, "Frankie, take it easy, you're going to turn the wagon over."

Victor grabbed the handle and stepped in front of Frankie. "I'm taking the wagon, you go slow and take care of your ankle."

He took their advice. "Fine, but I'm ready to get her home."

Al rubbed his neck and glanced toward the sky. "I know you had a rough landing due to not enough space to coast her down. Are you going to have enough room to take off?"

"I hope so. If not, I'll ask Mr. Johnson to take out part of his fence so we can get her on the road. It'll be an easy take off, but you and Victor will have to stop traffic."

Frankie checked the engine over and found a cracked fuel line. He replaced the line and readied the engine for a start. Al checked all of the cables, and Victor added gas to the tank. He climbed in while Victor propped the plane. The Jenny started on the first try. He let the engine run several minutes.

He stepped to the ground. "I'm going to take a walk through the pasture and see how much room I have to take off before I hit the pine thicket."

Frankie made his way to the tree line and gazed at the Jenny and then at the sky. He imagined where he would lift the plane off the ground and checked how much room he had before he hit the pine thicket. He didn't see a problem.

Victor and Al were waiting with the loaded wagon. Frankie walked toward the airplane and put on his hat and goggles. "I've got plenty of room to take off."

Al scratched his head. "Are you sure, son?"

He climbed in the plane. "Oh, yeah. I've taken off in a tighter area than this. Victor, prop me off and thank Mr. Johnson again."

Victor walked to the front of the plane and put his hands on the propeller. "I'll tell him. Be careful and we'll see you at the air field."

Frankie yelled, "Contact."

Victor responded, "Contact," then pulled down and stepped away. The engine started.

Frankie prayed and headed down the makeshift runway. He cleared the trees and watched Victor and Al wave. Normally he would do a trick for them, but he wanted to get his airplane home.

He arrived in Saplingville and put the Jenny in her shed. He limped to the hangar to start his work for the day.

Victor breezed out of his office at three o'clock. "Frankie, everything's quiet here, why don't you head home and rest."

He gathered tools. "I think I will. I'm going home, change clothes, and check on Ruthie. See you tomorrow."

He showered and changed into clean denim pants and a blue plaid shirt. He drove the few blocks to Ruthie's house. He spotted Ronald's light blue Studebaker parked on the street. He parked his Ford coupe behind Ronald's car. *What the hell?* Frankie heard Al's voice in his head, "Calm down, son, that temper of yours is as fiery as your hair."

He stared at the door handle and froze. He couldn't face being taken advantage of again. Ronald busted from the front door with Mrs. Douglas following. She stood on the porch with her hands on her hips.

Frankie jumped from his car and in two strides stood in front of the dandy. He towered over him and took advantage of the height difference.

Ronald raised his hands, stepped back, and almost lost his balance. "Hey, man, Ruth Ann told me about you two. She loves you. You can have her, she's replaceable."

Frankie raised his fist; he wanted to mess with the dandy's face. "Ruthie is irreplaceable to me. Now. Beat it. I don't want to see you or your blue car in Saplingville ever again. I'm not going to hurt your pretty face today, but if you give my girl a hard time or touch a hair on her head when she returns to school, I'll beat your ass."

The dandy backed his way to the car, opened the door, and jumped in.

When Ronald started his Studebaker, Frankie faced the house, Hattie stood in the door. "Mrs. Douglas, I'm sorry you had to witness the altercation. I lost my temper."

She hugged him and cried. "I'm glad you did, I just discovered what a despicable character he is. Do you know he wanted her to move to New York with him, unmarried? She set him straight and informed him that she loved you, she asked him to leave, and he started begging her. He said some other things I can't repeat. Ruth Ann knew I stood at the door listening, so she asked me to come in and escort him out. You arrived at the right time, Jacob's still at work."

He put his arm around Mrs. Douglas and guided her inside. "Everything's fine. He's gone for good, and I made sure he won't give Ruthie any problems when she returns to school."

"Thanks, Frankie, go on upstairs. She's upset."

He stood in the door and watched Ruthie cry into her pillow. "Can I come in?"

She got out of bed and ran. He cradled her in his arms. "Everything's fine. Ronald and I have an understanding. He won't hurt you again."

Her lips trembled. "But I have to go to school, he'll be there."

He stared into her face, wiping tears from her cheek with his thumb. "He won't bother you. I let him know I'd hurt his pretty face if he did."

Her eyes locked with his, and he recognized from this moment she would be his forever. Ronald's voice played through his head like a Victrola record, "She loves you."

He knelt on his right knee. "Ruth Ann Douglas." Frankie hesitated.

She frowned. "Does your ankle hurt?"

Frankie laughed trying to steady his nerves. "No, oh Dear God, help me. What I want is for us to get hitched. As soon as you get out of school, I want you to marry me. I'll never leave you. I'll adore you and take care of you. I'll do my best to be the man you deserve."

A large smile filled her face. "Frankie, I can't wait to marry you. I've loved you since you returned to Saplingville. Remember the hayride? When I gazed into your eyes I saw my future, although I didn't know it at the time."

He stood and gathered her in his arms and swung her around the room. Frankie whispered in her ear, "I'm going to make you so happy. We'll make love every night and have babies, if you want them."

She whispered in his ear, "I want them, but I can't wait to do what we do to get them."

He closed his eyes and reveled in the kiss she planted on his lips. She kissed him with more passion than anyone ever had, even Audrey. He'd never wanted another woman as much as he wanted her. He wouldn't have long to wait; she would be out of school in a few weeks.

She settled in the bed and smiled. "I'll talk to Ma, and we'll set the date for two weeks after graduation. Does that suit you?"

He grinned at his fiancée. "Suits me fine."

She smoothed her cover. "I want Lisbeth and Dottie as bridesmaids."

"Perfect, 'cause I want Victor and Al to be with me."

Hattie entered her room. "I'm fixing supper for you Frankie."

Ruthie raised her voice, "Ma, we have an announcement. Frankie proposed to me, and I accepted."

"Oh, thank God. Frankie, I couldn't ask for a better son-in-law than you." She folded her hands under her chin, happiness evident on her face.

He stood. "Do you think Mr. Douglas will be upset because I didn't ask his permission?"

"No, he already mentioned he hoped you two would get married. You already have his permission." She smiled and looked from her daughter to her future son-in-law.

Chapter Thirty-Five

Ruth Ann sat in bed studying pattern books. She flipped the page and recognized what she wanted. A picture of a model about her size in a simple sleeveless empire waist dress filled the page. "I like this one."

Delores took the book. "Yes, it's beautiful. I think the dress would be lovely made of ivory satin."

Hattie stood and gazed over Delores' shoulder. "Beautiful. Will you have enough time to make it?"

Ruth Ann's aunt studied the picture. "I don't see a problem. I'm glad you chose a simple one."

"Let's go to the store and get what we need." Hattie glanced at the clock. "It's early. Barringer's doesn't close for a couple of hours."

Delores dog-eared the page. "I need to get all of Ruth Ann's measurements before she goes back to school." She glanced at her niece. "I'll be back in a few days when you feel better, get your measurements, and show you the material and buttons."

Ruth Ann rose from her bed and paced the room. "Dottie and Lisbeth can wear one of their Sunday dresses. Frankie, Victor, and Al will wear their best suits." For the first time in years, she enjoyed spending time with her mother. "I'll help you with the cake and decorations when I get home."

Hattie shook her head. "No, I'll be fine. I don't want you to worry about a single thing. I'm planning to serve wedding cake, peanuts, candy mints, and punch for the reception. Lisbeth and I will decorate the gathering room."

She hugged her mother. "Thank you. I hope everyone will come to my graduation."

"Of course, we will except for Walter and Delores."

Delores stared at the floor. "We'll be there in spirit."

Hattie walked toward the door and turned and stared at her daughter. "Ruth Ann, I know we haven't gotten along in the last few years, and I'm sorry. I made some mistakes when I was young, but everything's fine now. I should have known everything would work for you, too. We learn from our mistakes. You'll know soon enough a mother wants what's best for her daughter."

Delores hugged her. "I'm so happy for you and Frankie. You couldn't have found a better man to marry than him."

"Thanks, Aunt Delores."

She heard the front door close and the screen door snap as her mother and Delores left for town. She counted the minutes until her barnstormer got off work.

Chapter Thirty-Six

Frankie wanted to kick his heels and run everywhere. His happiness and energy swept through the hangar to his friends. Al cleaned the hangar from top to bottom, and Victor finished paper work he'd stashed for three months.

He motioned for Al to join him in Victor's office. They sat in chairs opposite the boss. "I want you to stand with me when I marry. I want the two of you as my best men."

Victor and Al smiled at each other. Victor said, "I'd be honored to be one of your best men."

Al wiped a tear from his cheek. "Son, I've seen this day comin' for a long time. You and Victor are more like brothers than any I've ever seen. Now you will be, and you'll be marrying the girl you've always loved. I'm very proud of you, son."

He regarded the old man he loved so much. "Another thing, Al. Can my kids call you Grandpa Al?"

Al smiled, and his lips trembled. "You bet they can."

He glanced at Al and back to Victor. "I don't know what I would do without you two."

Victor said, "Why don't you take off early and spend time with Ruth Ann."

Frankie stood. "Thanks, I need to go by the jewelry store. Ruthie needs a ring on her finger before she returns to school. See you both in the morning."

He arrived at Price's Jewelry Store right before they closed.

Mr. Price cleaned the glass cases. "What can I help you with, Frankie?"

He searched the store until he spotted the ring counter. "I need an engagement and wedding ring. Ruthie and I are getting married."

Mr. Price placed several wedding sets on the counter. I'm not surprised. I remember Ruth Ann buying you the tie clip for Christmas."

Frankie chose a simple fourteen karat gold and platinum set with a small diamond. "I like this one." He checked the price. *Yep, in my price range.* "Do you have a plain wedding band for me? I'll buy it today, too."

Mr. Price said, "Good choice, I think she'll like this one. Yes, here's a popular men's wedding ring, a plain fourteen karat gold band."

He put the ring on his finger, a perfect fit. "Yes, I like the plain one, I do a lot of work with my hands, and I don't need anything fancy."

Mr. Price took the rings. "If Ruth Ann's set needs to be sized, I can do it here. May I gift wrap hers?"

"Yes, I'm going to give the engagement ring to her this afternoon, thanks."

Chapter Thirty-Seven

Ruth Ann stood at her window watching for Frankie. She couldn't stay in the bed one minute longer. She saw the Ford coupe turn in the driveway. She raced to her dresser, combed her hair, and pinched her cheeks before settling in bed. She fumbled with a book and pretended to read. She heard his footsteps on the stairs.

He knocked on her door. "Are you awake?"

"Of course. I can't sleep when it's time for you to come home. I can't wait until I'm waiting for you in our own house."

Frankie sat in the chair beside her bed and handed her the present. "This is for you, baby doll."

She reached for the box. "You bought me a present. What is it?"

"Open it and see."

She tore the paper off and opened the box. "Frankie, it's beautiful."

He pulled the box from her hands, removed the engagement ring, and placed Ruthie's left hand in his. He placed the ring on her finger. "Ruth Ann Douglas, with all my love, I give you this engagement ring. I can't wait to place the wedding ring on your finger."

She stared at the ring. "How did you know my size?"

"I didn't. Mr. Price said he'd resize if need be. Is it the correct size?"

She admired her ring. "Yes."

Frankie removed his from a pocket. "Let me show you mine." He placed it on his finger. "I wanted a plain gold band. Do you like it?"

She kissed the gold band gleaming on his left hand. "Yes, now all the women will know you're taken."

He leaned over to kiss her. "I've been taken for a long time."

Hattie peeked in the bedroom. "What's all the excitement? I can hear you in the kitchen."

She held her hand out. "See my engagement ring."

Hattie gazed at her pretty hand. "It's beautiful, Frankie. You did a great job picking it out." She stopped in the door before going downstairs. "I'm fixing enough supper for you, will you join us?"

He licked his lips in anticipation of the good food. "I sure will, Mrs. Douglas."

Hattie's voice softened, she gave Frankie a sincere smile. "We want you to call us Ma and Pa like our kids do. We're so proud you'll be part of this family."

He didn't know what to say, his chest swelled with pride. "That's an honor but may take me some time to get used to it."

With Hattie downstairs he plucked Ruthie from the bed and put her in his lap. She put her arms around his neck, and they kissed and held each other. He ran his hand under her gown, her smooth skin seared his heart with desire, his erection growing by the minute. He rolled her nipple between his fingers. She groaned and sucked his bottom lip between her teeth. He removed his hand and pulled her close placing tender kisses on her neck. He stood with her cradled in his arms and placed her in the bed. The vision of crawling into bed with her every night took his breath.

He sucked in air and sat in the chair. "We need to talk about some things."

She smoothed her hair. "What's on your mind?"

"About my house, I know it's small and not what you're used to."

She put her finger to his lips. "Stop, I'd live with you anywhere, even in the shanty house."

He relaxed in his chair. "I know we'll outgrow it when we have kids, but right now, it's all I've got."

"Right now, it's all we need. I love your house. I think it's cozy, and the closer I am to you, the better. I wanted to talk to you about something also."

He leaned closer and put his elbows on his knees giving her his full attention. "I'm listening."

"How do you feel about me working? You know I want a career. I don't want to be an actress in Hollywood or New York but I do want to act on stage and I'd like to teach. I hope to have my own theater someday." She stared at him waiting for his reply.

He kissed her on the cheek. "Baby doll, I would never take anything from you. I'll support you and help you all I can. But what about kids? I want kids, do you?"

She fumbled with her cover. "Of course, I can't wait to have your children. I talked to Ma, and she wants to be our babysitter."

"Sounds like you and Hattie are getting along better."

"We are, for the first time in years. Did you ask Victor and Al to be your best men?"

He settled in his chair and stretched his legs. "Yes, they both agreed. What shall I tell them to wear?"

"They can wear their Sunday suits. Dottie and Lisbeth are wearing their Sunday dresses." She tilted her head and smiled at him. "What are you going to wear?"

"I'm going to buy a new suit. What are you going to wear?" He gave her a devilish grin thinking about what she wouldn't be wearing on their wedding night.

"Not telling. It's bad luck for the groom to see the bride's dress before the wedding."

Frankie could not sit still, he jumped from his chair. "Ruthie, I can't believe you're marrying me. I'm the luckiest man in the world. I'm so excited I can't sleep, eat, or concentrate on my work. Baby doll, you are making me crazy!"

She climbed out of bed and snuggled her head on Frankie's chest. "You are making me crazy, and I have to finish school and take final exams. Now, kiss me."

He lifted her off the floor. She held on tightly and nestled her face in his neck and inhaled his scent. Today he smelled like spice and soap. She laughed.

He released her. "What's so funny?"

"I'm laughing at the thought of a man smelling like Pond's Extract Vanishing Cream."

"What brought that to mind?"

"You." She put her finger on his chest. "You smell like spice and soap, and I like it. Now, kiss me, again."

Chapter Thirty-Eight

Ruth Ann met Frankie at the door with her suitcases. She tiptoed and kissed him wrapping her arms around his neck. "Let's go. I'm ready to get this school work done so I can come home. I miss you already."

He placed her bags in the car. "After we're married, I will not spend even one day without you in my bed."

She felt the same aching in the pit of her stomach she always experienced when Frankie stood next to her, but when he mentioned bed, it was if an electric current swept through her body. "Frankie Howard, you are some kind of a man, you have no idea what you do to me."

He winked. "I crave you like a man dying of thirst in a desert."

She smiled and winked. "In a few weeks' time, you will never be thirsty again."

Hattie breezed out to the porch and hugged them. "Be careful. Ruth Ann, call me collect, when you get to Atlanta."

She hugged her mother. "I will, see you at graduation."

She scooted over in the front seat and sat as close to Frankie as she could. The ride to Andrew's Field quick, she spotted the large black airplane with gold trim sitting on the runway. "Are you flying this one today?"

"Yes, ma'am. I know you're nervous about flying again, and I wanted you to be comfortable. The Stinson Trimotor has three engines and lots of room."

She climbed in the airplane seat, fastened her seat belt, and waited for Frankie to finish his pre-flight check list. The plane appeared much larger than the other planes and had more gauges.

He settled in his seat and started the engines. "What do you think?"

She ran her hand over the instruments encased in glass. "This is amazing, but how do you know what each of these gauges are for?"

He taxied down the runway. "It's not complicated. I can explain them to you."

She shook her head. "No, I don't need to know, as long as you and Victor know what you're doing. And Lisbeth, too, I keep forgetting she's going to be a pilot. How's she doing in her lessons?"

"Fine, as anything else she does. She's a very smart girl. Both of you are."

"How fast does this thing go?"

He checked the gauges giving his full attention to the task at hand. "Our cruising speed will be around one hundred twenty-five miles per hour. You'll be in Atlanta in no time."

She settled in for the flight, and soon they landed at Candler Field. The plane made her feel safe, along with her trust in Frankie.

He parked the plane. "I promised your mother I'd ride with you in the taxi to the school and make sure you get settled."

She unfastened her seatbelt. "I can't wait for you to see the school and where I've lived for the last eight months."

He helped her out of her seat. "Find us a taxi. I need to talk to the ground crew. I want them to put gas in the plane while I'm gone."

The taxi stopped in front of her living quarters. Frankie leaned toward the front seat. "Can you wait for five minutes? I won't be long."

She opened the door to her apartment, and they stepped inside. "Nice place. Where do you want your suitcase?"

"Just here. I'll take care of it." She grabbed his hand not wanting to let him go. "I wish you would stay with me."

Frankie scrutinized the small space. "Precious, if I stayed here alone with you, things would happen. I've got to go. If you need me, if the dandy says anything out of the way or bothers you, call me." He gathered her in his arms and kissed her until he felt her desire rise to meet his. "I love you, and I'll see you in two weeks at graduation."

Her legs shifted to jelly. When he sat her on the floor, she grabbed his arm to steady herself.

He pulled her close. "Are you all right?"

She put her head against his chest. "I'm fine. You make me feel weak in the knees."

He kissed the top of her head. "I hope I always will."

She watched Frankie make his way to the taxi taking her heart with him. He waved, she smiled and waved. She missed him already.

Chapter Thirty-Nine

Frankie entered the semi-dark theater with Ruthie's family. Sadness filled his heart when he saw the stage. He regretted not seeing her performance in the play, but at least he could attend her graduation. Jacob, Hattie, Victor, Dottie, Lisbeth, and Frankie sat close to the front. Soon the 1937 graduating class of the Atlanta Theatre of the Arts took their seats on stage. The President of the College called Ruth Ann Douglas. She walked to the podium to receive her certificate. The Douglas family jumped to their feet. Jacob whooped and hollered the loudest.

Frankie whistled and yelled, "That's *my* girl."

After the ceremony, he ran to the stage and grabbed Ruthie, kissed her, and hugged her close. "Now, you're coming home with me."

She kissed him. "I didn't think these two weeks would ever end."

Ronald and Jenny Price made their way through the crowd toward them. He put a protective arm around Ruthie.

Ronald put his hand out. "Congratulations, I hear you're engaged."

Frankie shook Ronald's hand and grinned when he winced from his handshake. "Thank you. We're getting married in two weeks."

Ronald put his arm around the girl. "This is Jenny

Price she's going with me to New York. We leave Monday morning."

Frankie and Ruth Ann burst out laughing. Ruth Ann controlled her laughter and peered at the confused pair. "Good luck in New York. I hope you both make it big."

Before everyone boarded the flight to Saplingville, Jacob pulled Ruth Ann and Frankie aside. "For your graduation present, your mother and I found a place for rent on Main Street. We believe it would be perfect for the little theater you want to develop. We'll pay the first three month's rent, and then you're on your own. It's going to need some work. You'll have to build a stage and any rooms you need for teaching."

She threw her arms around her daddy and kissed his cheek. "Pa, thank you."

Frankie shook Jacob's hand. "Thank you, sir. I can build anything Ruthie needs. I know Al will help me."

Jacob nodded. "You and my daughter make a good pair. You're both stubborn enough to succeed at anything you want to do."

Victor flew the Stinson Trimotor with Lisbeth in the co-pilot's seat. Frankie sat with his girl and held her hand. As soon as they landed, they joined the rest of the family along with Al and Ethel at Walter and Delores' farm for supper.

Chapter Forty

Frankie rose early on the day of his wedding. He'd made a promise to himself to visit the cemetery. He placed some daisies on his mama's grave and sat on the bench he'd placed near the headstone several years ago. "Mama, I wish you were here. I know I've made some mistakes and haven't been the man you wanted me to be, but things are good now. I'm getting married today to someone you would approve of and love. She loves me Mama, and she makes me a better man." He let the tears come, he hadn't cried since the day they buried her. "Bye, Mama, next time I visit, I'll have my wife with me."

He drove his car home and spent the morning cleaning their little house. The four-room house consisted of a bedroom, front room, kitchen, and bathroom. He couldn't be prouder, if he lived in a mansion. Compared to where he'd lived, it was. The pink rose bush planted by former occupants stood laden with blooms. Frankie grabbed some scissors and a mason jar. He filled the jar with as many roses as he could cram in and topped it off with water. He placed the jar on the table next to the bed. Everything in the house sparkled waiting for the lady of the house to arrive.

Frankie placed his black and white pin stripe suit and vest on his bed. He removed his white shirt from the hangar and placed it on the chair along with his black and white tie. He searched through a small drawer for his tie clip. He stared at the image of the biplane and kissed it for luck. He'd come full circle. He left Saplingville at fifteen to follow his barnstormer dream. He didn't regret his false starts and bad luck. He wouldn't be the man he is today if those things never happened. Frankie closed his eyes and thanked God for leading him to this moment.

He took a cola bottle from the icebox and headed to his front porch. His knotted stomach made it impossible to eat lunch. He sat in the front porch swing nursing his drink. He rolled the empty bottle between his hands. His thoughts were of his wedding and his new bride. He wouldn't spend another lonely day in this house, and his life would never be quiet with Ruthie beside him.

Chapter Forty-One

Ruth Ann stared in her bedroom mirror while Lisbeth pinned flowers in her black bobbed hair. "Do you think I have on enough make-up?"

Lisbeth kept working but studied her face. "A little more rouge. Are you wearing red lipstick?"

She smiled and showed her sister the tube. "Red Hot Red to match my fingernails."

Lisbeth combed the back of her hair. "Frankie's going get your lipstick on him when he kisses you."

"He won't care as long as he gets to kiss me."

Hattie hurried in the room holding her wedding gown. "Time to put on your dress. Lisbeth, Ruth Ann's hair is beautiful. I love the flowers."

She stood and removed her robe.

Her mother held out the dress, and Ruth Ann stepped into it. Hattie fastened the row of satin buttons down the back. "You are beautiful."

Lisbeth stared. "You *are* beautiful. I'm very happy for you and Frankie. I hope I find someone as good as Frankie is to you and Dottie is to Victor."

Jacob waited by the front door for his daughter. He smiled when he saw her float down the stairs. "My, my, don't you look beautiful."

Her lower lip trembled. "Thanks, Pa."

Jacob placed her in the front seat. She smoothed her dress to prevent wrinkles. Hattie and Lisbeth sat in the rear seat. Jacob started the Buick and headed to the church.

She stared out the window of the car. She'd traveled these roads many times, but the houses and yards appeared different. Her senses on high alert, she saw her world for the first time. Her hands shook as if she were about to go on stage. She closed her eyes and practiced her breathing technique. Her belly expanded against the smooth satin dress and her heart beat returned to normal. The car stopped in front of the church.

Dottie opened her door. "Ruth Ann, you are stunning. Take my hand, I'll help you out."

She grasped Dottie's hand. "Hurry, Frankie can't see me."

Hattie hugged her. "Go with Dottie and Lisbeth. I have to stay here."

She grabbed her mother and hugged her tightly. "Thanks, Ma. I love you."

Hattie held her daughter and whispered, "I love you, too."

The three girls hurried to an empty Sunday School room. Ruth Ann stood by the window. "How long do we wait?"

Dottie sat in a chair. "Pa will come and get us when it's time."

Chapter Forty-Two

Frankie, Victor, and Al waited together. At two o'clock they left the room and walked to the church sanctuary. Mrs. Wilson played 'Oh Promise Me' while the men and bridesmaids entered the church. When the men were in their places, she pounded an F-chord and started the 'Bridal Chorus.'

Frankie's heart raced at the sight of his bride. She looked like an angel. *My beautiful angel.* Al patted him on the back, and he regained his composure.

Jacob marched her to the front of the church, placed her hand in his, and declared he and Henrietta were giving their daughter to him.

His heart pounded, and he willed himself to breathe. Lisbeth stepped to the piano. He held Ruthie's hand, and after a cue from Lisbeth, he started singing "The Shadow Waltz."

He gazed into his bride's eyes and sang. Ruthie fingered the heart pendant he gave her for Christmas. Hattie sobbed and Jacob put his arm around his wife. Frankie nodded toward them. When the song ended, he brushed Ruthie's tears from her cheek and kissed her on the forehead.

Pastor Lowe said, "Not so fast, let's say the vows first." After the giggles and laughter subsided, Pastor Lowe started the ceremony. "Dearly Beloved, we are gathered here today in the sight of God and these witnesses to join Francis Jack Howard and Ruth Ann Douglas in holy matrimony."

They repeated their vows, exchanged rings, and sealed everything with a kiss. After the long kiss that had Pastor Lowe clearing his throat and the men of the congregation cheering, he dug in his pocket for a handkerchief to wipe the lipstick off his face. Everyone clapped and laughed.

Ruthie said, "Frankie, you're wiping off my kiss."

"No, I'm wiping off your lipstick. Figured you'd be wearing the same color as your nails."

They strolled through the aisle to applause and waited while people gathered in the large reception room.

Carol Ann and Jack Andrew ran to Frankie. He held them one in each arm, and Ruthie kissed their cheeks. Victor grabbed them before they ripped the flowers from her hair.

Victor said, "All right, you two, let Uncle Frankie and Aunt Ruth Ann enjoy their day. We'll take you to their house and leave you with them when they return from their honeymoon."

She swung her head toward her husband causing a daisy to topple out of her hair. "Honeymoon?"

He put his arm around her. "Yep, but it's a surprise. We're leaving tomorrow and no, I'm not telling you where we're going."

She squeezed his arm. "But I haven't packed. I planned to get my clothes from home and take to your house next week. I have enough for the next few days."

Frankie bent his head and rested his forehead on hers. "Don't worry, wife. Lisbeth took care of everything. By the time we get home, your suitcases will be waiting for us."

The reception ended, and everyone threw rice as they ran to Frankie's car. When they arrived home, he scooped her in his arms and carried her through the front door. He kicked the door closed and made his way to the bedroom turning sideways as he entered with Ruthie still in his arms.

He continued to hold her and they kissed until she slipped her feet to the floor. "Unbutton these buttons, please."

Frankie stared at the row of buttons. "You've got to be kidding me. You're not making this easy, are you?"

She laughed. "I'm worth waiting for."

He had already gotten half way down her back with the buttons. "Yes, you are, Mrs. Howard."

She stepped out of the dress and draped it on a chair.

Frankie watched her. "Do you have any idea how beautiful you are?"

She unfastened each garter and rolled her stockings down her legs. She stood, tugged his coat off, and unbuttoned his vest. She loosened his tie and started on his shirt buttons. "Do you have any idea how handsome you are?" He shivered as Ruthie unfastened his belt and pants.

She tugged his pants and drawers at the same time. She gazed from the top of his head to his toes. "You're even more handsome with no clothes on." She ran her hands over his muscles and buried her head in the softness of the hairs on his chest.

He reached for her slip straps and let them fall as he tugged the garment until it fell to the ground. "My turn to undress you." He stared at his bride, her beauty took his breath away. He kissed her and drew her close. He wanted to feel her bare skin against his. He unfastened her brassiere and threw it over his shoulder. He pulled her close, her nipples hardened against his body. He bent and kissed her from her neck to her soft breasts as he shoved her panty briefs until they hit the floor, and she stepped out of them. He held her, the feel of her soft body against him ignited a passion he didn't know existed. "I love you." The words came easy now.

She returned the words in a whisper. "I love you, too."

He picked her up and placed her on the bed. He'd vowed to go slow, take his time, make sure she enjoyed every second. He started his quest to memorize every part of her before the night was over. Only when he had pleased her enough times she begged for him inside her did he give in to his own need. A need, if he lived, only his precious Ruthie would fill.

****

Sunshine burned into the house when Frankie opened his eyes. He glanced at his alarm clock, ten in the morning. Ruthie's head rested on his chest, his arm under her and her arm and leg draped over his body. He stayed in bed listening to her soft snores remembering their first night as husband and wife. He didn't have the heart to wake her. They stayed awake until the wee hours. He lost count of how many times they made love. Just when he thought they'd had enough and settled in each other's arms, a touch or a kiss or a word had them loving each other again. When they rested, they talked, making plans for their life. He removed his body from hers. She didn't wake, she pivoted to her side. He put on his drawers and walked to the kitchen to make coffee and breakfast.

Ruthie entered the kitchen wearing his white shirt. "Good morning."

Frankie raked his eyes over his bride, picked her up and cradled her in his arms. "Good morning, my shirt looks better on you. I hoped you'd sleep a little longer."

She wrapped her arms around his neck. "I smelled bacon and coffee. Besides I'm excited about our honeymoon. Where are you taking me?"

Frankie swung around holding her close. "We're going to Tybee Island for a little fun in the sun." He let her legs fall to the floor.

She put her arms around his neck. "I love Tybee Island."

He kissed her. "I know."

She kissed his neck. "I don't think we'll be seeing much of the sun or the beach."

A smile filled Frankie's face, one that would never fade as long as he had her. "If we don't, I'll take you another time. We've got the rest of our lives."

A word about the author...

Before fulfilling her dream of being a published romance writer, Jane Lewis worked as a free-lance musician and teacher, and an analyst and manager for a large railroad company. She is a native of Atlanta and lover of all things southern. She graduated from Kennesaw State University, Kennesaw, Georgia, with a Bachelor of Arts degree in Music.

When she isn't writing her next romance, she enjoys cooking, tending her rose garden, playing music, yoga, and bowling with her real life hero, her husband. She and her husband live in a suburb outside of Atlanta.

She is a member of Romance Writers of America, Georgia Romance Writers and Georgia Writers Association. She was a 2016 finalist in the Hearts Through History, Post-Victorian/World War II category for her first romance novel, *Love at Five Thousand Feet*.

Website: www.janelewisauthor.com
Facebook https://www.facebook.com/janelewisauthor/
Twitter https://twitter.com/janelewisauthor
Pinterest https://www.pinterest.com/janelewis9917/